DILEMMAS OF A DAMSEL

Part II

Monique Elise

ISBN: 1732075700
ISBN-13: 978-1732075702

"You've got to learn to leave the table when the love is no longer being served..."

- Nina Simone

ACKNOWLEDGMENTS

My deepest thank you to everyone that has continued to support my work. You guys are the best! Ten years ago, I never would've imagined creating something that I hold so close and dear to my heart. I have a strong suspicion that this is only the beginning! This story is for anyone that has ever been betrayed by someone they loved. Don't let heartbreak break you.

PROLOGUE

She gasps at the tiny prick in her skin before slowly dragging the sharp razor blade across her wrist. Small drops of blood trickle into the bathroom sink. The feeling of relief that rushes over her is soothing.

She needed a release, an escape, even if it was only for a moment. She closes her eyes and bites her bottom lip as a single tear rolls down her cheek. Today was not a good day. After arguing with her mother and new boyfriend, she needed a way to channel her anger. Once she opens her eyes, she struggles to look at herself in the mirror. Shame was beginning to settle in; she hated when she did this to herself.

Normally when she felt like the pressures of her thirteen-year-old life were getting to be too much, she'd curl up into her shell and get lost in her dreams. She'd imagine being rescued by her prince charming, traveling around the world on grand ships and magic carpets. She always loved a good fairy tale; for her, it was an alternative to her reality. Fairy tales gave her a chance to take control and remove the misery she felt existed in her life. In fairy tales, there are only happy-endings. In fairy tales, the love never dies.

A soft knock on the door breaks her out of her trance.

"Blair are you ready? We'll be leaving in five minutes!" her mother Camille calls out.

Blair protests, "I'm not coming!"

She can hear her mother sigh on the other side of the door.

"I promise I will call your father this evening to discuss you staying with him for a bit. But right now we have reservations for lunch that we don't want to miss. Please hurry up," Camille pleads.

Blair despised living in Arizona; it was so slow and far too hot compared to her beloved Philadelphia. She hated that her mother dragged her across the country when her parents split up. Even more, she hated Gerald, her mother's boyfriend and a constant thorn in her side. It's not that he was a bad person, per se, but he wasn't her father Quincy, and in her eyes, he was one of the reasons why her parents have not reconciled.

From the moment her parents divorced, she felt like something was missing. Being shuffled among them tortured her, and she longed for things to be different. She loved them both, and she hated feeling like she had to choose between them.

She reaches for a rag and applies pressure to her open wound to stop the bleeding. After patching it up with a bandage, she goes into her bedroom and throws on her favorite long-sleeve orange sweatshirt to hide her secret.

At lunch, she remains numb; eating her chicken fingers in silence, and all but ignoring her mother and Gerald. Camille knew that the sudden change took a toll on her daughter. But it's been six months; she figured Blair would've adjusted by now. Regardless, she felt guilty for uprooting her so suddenly. Deep down, she worried that her decision to do so changed her daughter forever. Blair was usually so happy, so bright, like walking sunshine. But slowly over the last few months, that light has dimmed. She was desperate to bring her vibrant little girl back; she was so curious and adventurous, full of life and imagination. Camille knew she had so much to offer the world. In an attempt to smooth things over, Blair's mother suggests taking a stroll to get some ice cream after lunch. She knew that strawberry ice cream with sprinkles was something her daughter couldn't refuse.

Blair enjoys her ice cream cone and follows Camille and Gerald as they walk hand in hand through the flea market taking place in the neighborhood. She checks out the antiques and used goods being sold by the locals, but nothing seems to impress her. That's until she comes across a table containing various hand-painted sketches and pictures. Her fingers trail the beautifully crafted pieces until her eyes settle on a peculiar painting. Something about it draws her in immediately; she never saw anything like it. It was a butterfly on fire. Blair doesn't know if it's the colors, the symbolism, or what; but something was awoken inside of her. Her heart starts to race with excitement.

"How much for this?" she asks the hippie vendor.

"Five bucks," the kind woman says.

Luckily for Blair, she received her allowance before the blow-up earlier that day. She quickly reaches into her back pocket and pulls out a crumpled up five-dollar bill before passing it off. Her face lights up as the vendor places the painting in a plastic bag and hands it to her.

Camille is a few feet away at another display containing an array of handcrafted jewelry. Her eyes quickly scan the crowd in search of Blair. When she sees her, she relaxes a bit.

She summons her, "Honey, come check out these cool earrings!"

Camille watches her daughter with curiosity. As Blair gets closer, she doesn't know if it was the ice cream or the afternoon sun, but something was different about her.

BLAIR

1

I love my boyfriend so much! This was the thought that crossed my mind not so long ago. But it's amazing how fast things can change. One minute you're ecstatic, loving life. Then, all it takes is one instant to make it all come crashing down. In my case, only a few moments ago I was a woman in love, celebrating my thirtieth birthday with the ones I loved most. That all changed with seven simple words. *"I'm the one carrying your child."*

That sentence plays over and over again in my head. Each time it does, I can feel a part of my heart shatter into pieces. My boyfriend cheated on me, and the other woman is having his baby. She's having a baby with my man, my world. Guess the jokes on me right? *How could he do this to me?*

I can't stand the sight of them. But the harsh new reality of my life leaves me feeling paralyzed. I try with all of my might to find my voice; I want to yell, and I want to confront them. I just want to make it all go away, but I'm stuck. As my subconscious continues to scream for me to do something, he suddenly pulls her in for a hug, and my chest tightens. My head spins, and nausea forces me to cower towards the bathroom covering my mouth. I quickly enter the bathroom stall and lean my head over the toilet, throwing up everything that's inside of me, even my heart. The bathroom door opens once more, and I try to silence my sobbing.

"Blair, are you in here?" Jade calls out.

I silently curse myself.

I hear Kara say, "I swear that I saw her run in here!"

I hold my breath, hoping that they'll give up and return to the party. But a few seconds later, I can see their heels in front of my stall. There's a soft knock on the door, but I remain quiet, too embarrassed to face them.

"We can see your feet," Jade announces.

I sigh and reluctantly reach up to open the door. Their eyes meet mine, and it's as if they've seen a ghost. I'm a mess, curled up on the bathroom floor with tears streaming down my face.

"Oh my god!" Kara shouts.

Jade is by my side at once, "What happened?"

I can't even get the words out. It feels like there is a huge rock in my throat.

All I can manage to say is, "Jayson, her, baby."

They quickly put two and two together and promptly

jump into damage control. I can barely keep my balance when they help me up off the ground. They carry me over to the mirror and work to put me back together; fixing my hair, wiping my face, and reapplying my lipstick. When they finish, they wait for my next move.

"What do you want to do?" Jade asks.

"Get me out of here," I whimper.

Without hesitation, my friends guide me outside to the valet and retrieve Jade's Audi. Once it arrives, they help me into the front seat. Jade quickly starts the car and blasts the AC to cool me off before turning back towards the building.

She orders, "Kara, stay with her. I'm going to go inside to get her things."

Kara nods, "Got it."

I sink into the cool leather seat as Kara joins me inside the car. In an attempt to briefly take my mind off of things, she reaches over and turns on some music. I look at her and just want to cry. I was so lucky to have her and Jade as friends, especially at this exact moment. I needed them more than they could ever know.

Out of the corner of my eye, I see Jayson come out of the venue and approach the car. I flinch at the mere sight of him. He takes one look at me, and I can see the dread overcome his face, he knows something is wrong. I don't want to hear his voice, let alone see him.

He knocks on the curbside window, "Blair, what's going on?"

I ignore him, crossing my arms and focusing on the car's dashboard. He refuses to back down and walks over to the passenger side of the car and opens the door.

"Babe, what's wrong?" he repeats.

Once again, hot tears stream down my face, "Don't worry about me, worry about Renee and your unborn child!"

His face sinks. I can tell that he's trying to think of what to say.

After a moment he turns his attention to Kara, "Do you mind giving us a minute?"

Kara ignores him and looks at me, "You good Blair?"

I softly pat her hand. She gives me a knowing smile and slightly bows her head.

"I'll be right here ok?" Kara reassures me.

I nod before I get out the car and face the man that jaded me. He can see the pain all over my face. My eyes are swollen and red from crying while Jayson's looks strained and weary.

He begins, "Please let me explain."

The sound of his voice instantly gets under my skin. I want to jump on him and let him feel the extent of my wrath.

I wipe away my tears and say, "I don't need you to explain shit! What are you going to say? Huh? How you ended up cheating on me or how you ended up getting her pregnant?"

I can see the valet attendants stop and glance over at us. The last thing I want to do is cause a scene, but I can't help myself. The more he talked, the more I can feel my skin boiling over with rage. This type of betrayal is unforgivable.

He tries to pull me in for a hug, "I know that I messed up, but let me fix this."

"You can't fix this!" I quickly push him away, avoiding his advances, "I hate you!"

Before I know it, I'm breaking down. My sorrow takes complete control over my body and causes me to drop to my knees. Jayson reaches out trying to console me once more before I slap his hands away. Kara instantly jumps out of the car and helps me up.

"Blair please," Jayson begs.

At that moment, Jade rejoins us and comes to my side. She cuts her eyes at Jayson refusing to acknowledge his existence.

She orders, "Let's go y'all."

And again, my girlfriends give me support and help me into the car, leaving Jayson, his deceit and all of his lies on the curb. I crawl into the backseat and take a sip of the water Jade brought me. I lie back and close my eyes, clinging to my clutch and birthday gifts. I can still hear Jayson outside of Jade's car, but his pleading falls on deaf ears.

Jade says, "She doesn't want to talk to you right now."

"This is none of your damn business Jade," he sneers.

She doesn't back down, "If you say so. That bill wasn't any of my business either, but I gladly gave the bartender your name and phone number. I'd take care of that if I were you."

Without saying another word, she joins Kara and me in the car before pulling off.

At Jade's place, I'm numb. My thoughts are clouded by hurt, confusion, and disbelief. The day plays over and over again in my mind. From being surprised by Jayson with breakfast in bed, to making love all morning, to him then taking me shopping and treating me to lunch in the afternoon. My birthday started out so fucking good. I can't get over how quickly it all came crashing down. It's like a nightmare that I can't wake up from, no matter how hard I try.

Kara takes a seat beside me, interrupting my internal agony for a brief moment. She remains tight-lipped but places her hand on mine. Jade joins us after changing into something more comfortable. She quietly takes a seat on the floor in front of me, crossing her legs Indian-style. I can feel their eyes on me and can sense their apprehension, they are both scared of what to say or do next. Blu, Jade's cat, joins us, getting comfortable on my lap as I mindlessly stroke his white and toffee colored fur. Recollecting the last hour or so of my life was not something I looked forward to.

Kara finally asks, "So what the hell happened?"

I let out a heavy sigh and divulge every aching detail. My friends can't help but to look as horrified and enraged as I feel. They hold nothing back when expressing their disapproval of the situation. Normally I'd speak up to defend Jayson and his shady ways, but not this time. I just can't.

"Oh my goodness he's such an asshole!" Kara criticizes.

Jade digs, "So you mean to tell me; he let you have your birthday party at that place, knowing his side chick was working there the whole fucking time?"

"He is so disgusting!" Kara continues to fume.

"Blair you deserve so much better," Jade adds.

I knew that he wasn't high up on Jade or Kara's list of favorite people, but hearing them drag Jayson through the dirt so easily didn't feel that good either. This was a man that I thought I was going to marry. That's something that I just can't handle right now, so I decide to keep those thoughts to myself. My phone rings and I grab it out of my clutch. When I see Jayson's name come across the screen, I swiftly hit ignore.

I look at my friends, "I don't know what hurts more, the fact that he lied, or got another woman pregnant."

As soon as the words leave my mouth, another round of sobs escape me, and I have a complete meltdown.

It's been two days, and all I've managed to do is put a dent in Jade's expensive couch. Jayson has called and texted nonstop, but I can't deal with him right now. I just wasn't ready to face him, because facing him makes it all real. After getting all of the disapproval off their chests,

Jade and Kara tried being as supportive and understanding as they could. Luckily, Jade welcomed me with open arms and gave me free reign of her apartment. Considering that all of my clothes and belongings are back at the home I share with Jayson; she was more than accommodating. Kara made sure to call in and check on me, even dropping off a few toiletries, underwear and other necessities she thought I'd need.

I spend my days sleeping, crying and trying to piece together my life. Sleep helps me the most. But each time I open my eyes and don't see, hear, or feel Jayson next to me, my heart sinks back into my stomach, and my world comes crashing down once more.

When the tears seem to have settled, I'm anxious to write down all of my feelings. Usually, when I'm down, writing helps me to see things clearly. In an effort to make sense of all the chaos in my head I search for something to write with. I find a piece of paper and loose pen on Jade's desk and try to make sense of my thoughts. After fifteen minutes of starting then stopping and starting over again, I crumble the paper up and toss it onto the floor. Defeated, I reach for the remote and turn on the television.

After catching up on the latest season of *Queen Sugar*, I pull myself up off the couch and decide to do something productive, like take a shower. In the bathroom, I strip off my clothes and stand in front of the mirror. I look unrecognizable; my hair is a mess, and my eyes are puffy and bloodshot red. My chocolate skin doesn't seem to have its usual luster.

In the shower, Renee, Jayson, and our relationship rush through my mind. I try figuring out what went wrong. I can remember our first date like it was yesterday. Once upon a time, I felt like I was so lucky to be Jayson's girlfriend, proud even. The thought of him being with another woman is unbearable. Trying to make sense of this kind of betrayal felt impossible. To make matters worse, she's pregnant, pregnant by the love of my fucking life. I was the one that was supposed to be having his child. Something I've dreamed of for so many nights. The fact that he allowed someone to take that away from me makes me feel like I'm dying inside. I love him with all of my heart, and I longed to be everything he ever wanted. I can't help but wonder why he had to go looking elsewhere. *Was I not enough? Was something wrong with me?*

I lean my back up against the shower and close my eyes, trying my best to fight back my tears. I look down at my wrist, and a small scar stares back at me. Memories of that dark time in my life rush through my mind. I never thought I'd feel the urge to cut again, but I feel like I'm standing on the edge of a cliff. *How am I supposed to get through this?* Against my will, the deep agonizing cry living inside me finally comes to the surface, and I can't fight it any longer. I let it out and sink to my knees hoping the shower water will drown out my pain.

After drying off, I relentlessly try to pull myself together. I comb through my hair and gather it into a bun. I walk into Jade's bedroom and grab a pair of her yoga pants, a t-shirt, and sneakers. *I need to get out of this apartment.* I haven't been outside in days, and I desperately need some fresh air. I've been hiding from the world for far too long. Once outside, the sun feels good on my skin. It's bright and hopeful, things I long to feel again. I opt to walk around the corner and go to the Italian Deli for a snack. I haven't eaten much in days but suddenly can't think of anything but food.

If I allowed myself to admit it, I've had my suspicions for a while. Of course, I noticed he was staying out later and being more private with his phone. My intuition was screaming at me, and I chose to be blind to it. Instead, I convinced myself that I was being insecure; something Jayson often accused me of. Not wanting to continue to push the issue, I swallowed my pride to keep the peace. I wanted to trust that what we had was good. Maybe if I were more loving and attentive to him and his needs, this would've never happened.

At the deli, I take a seat at the counter and pull out my phone as I wait for my turkey club. My phone is filled with countless texts and notifications from Jayson and my other friends. I go to my Instagram and see all the pictures from my birthday party. My heart skips when I notice Renee in one of the pictures. She's in the corner, scowling at Jayson and me while I naively pose for a picture. I quickly close my phone and slam it down. The more I think about it, the more I feel myself getting pissed off. The cashier brings me my sandwich and Dr. Pepper, briefly interrupting my thoughts.

The next day, I feel anxious, pondering my next move. I know that I can't hide out at Jade's forever. And now that she and Max have reconciled, I'm starting to feel like I'm getting in the way of things. I would've gladly stayed at Kara's but her brother is visiting from out of town, and I didn't want to be a burden there either. I've never felt so out of place in my life; I hated to impose on others.

I try to get comfortable on the couch. Then I notice my blue gift bag from Tiffany's along with other gifts and cards that I completely forgot about. Lord knows these were the furthest things from my mind. Looking at them, I feel guilty for completely neglecting them. I stand to retrieve my presents from the glass shelf before plopping back down onto the couch. I reach inside the Tiffany's bag, a gift from Jade, and pull out a small blue box, wrapped in a white bow. I slightly smile before opening it and gasp at the beautiful sterling silver bangle with personalized engraving.

The words read, "*You are magical.*"

Through my agony, I can't help but smile. Suddenly, I feel compelled to express my appreciation for everything she's done for me. I quickly pull out my phone and call her.

She answers on the third ring, "Blair? Is everything ok?"

"Yes, I'm fine. I just wanted to thank you for my gift, it's perfect," I say.

She sounds relieved, "Oh! I'm so glad you like it."

"I do. I also wanted to thank you for you know, helping me out right now," I continue.

"Of course girl, you know I'll always have your back," she replies.

I exhale, "That means so much to me. I know how you like having your space, I'll try to be out of your way soon enough."

"No rush! I'm going to stay over at Max's house tonight, so the place is all yours," she insists.

The fact that they were picking right back up where they left off cheered me up, if only for a moment.

I boast, "I'm so glad to see you two back together."

I can hear her smile through the phone, "Me too!"

"Ok, I'll talk to you later," I say.

"Are you alright? Do you need me to bring anything? Do you want food or wine? I can stop at the store before I come home to change and grab a few things," she offers.

"No thank you, I'm good."

"K boo! See you soon," she says before we hang up.

I put my phone down and stare at the floor. In an attempt to center my thoughts, I search for another piece of blank paper and a pen. Finding a blank notebook on Jade's desk, I take a seat on the couch and begin writing.

Beautifully broken,
You came in and had me open.
Why isn't my love good enough?
I tried to be everything you ever wanted and desired.
But you keep breaking my heart, and I'm tired.
You say you're sorry and will never do it again.
But here I am broken.

I stop writing and pick my phone up once more. I check all of my unanswered texts and voicemails; most of them are from Jayson. He still hasn't stopped calling or texting me. I ignore them all; I still wasn't ready to face it. Part of me, however, is relieved. It felt good to know that he still cared.

I look at all of the pictures and videos documenting our love and wonder if it all was a lie. My mind sifts through all the memories we share, trying to pinpoint where things went wrong. *How the hell did I get here?*

I sit there in silence for a few moments before I open our text thread and see over fifty unread text messages. As expected, Jayson is full of apologies, all out begging for my forgiveness, promising to make things right. I scroll through them, unsure of how to reply.

I sit in contemplation. Stuck in a dilemma of following my heart or listening to my head. Deep down I want to believe him; I want to believe that some of what we had was good. I put in way too much time, effort and tears into this relationship. I refuse to let some young chick come in and take all of the glory. This is my relationship, my life; I have to fight for it. I'm the one that Jayson is supposed to be with; I'm the one that should be having his babies. This isn't right.

I weave my fingers through my hair and massage my scalp, trying to put my mind at ease. If I allow myself to admit it, I miss him more than I should. Confusion is an understatement. I go to my voicemail and see ten unopened messages. I open the most recent one, left this morning, and place my phone up to my ear.

"Blair, I know I fucked up. But I love you, and I know that we can work through this. Please don't give up on us. I'll do whatever it takes to get you back. I need you," I hear Jayson say and can tell he's fighting back tears.

I put my phone down and break down once more, crying myself to sleep. Before I know it, I'm awakened by the sound of keys in the door. Jade comes in, and she's glowing. She gives me a hug before quickly hopping into the shower. After about twenty minutes and failing to go back to sleep, I pull myself up off the couch and walk into her bedroom. She's changed into a form-fitting nude dress, swapping her conservative Jimmy Choo heels for sexy strappy sandals. I lay on her bed playing with Blu while she does her makeup.

After applying her blush, Jade turns to look at me, "You sure you don't want to come with us to dinner?"

I quickly shake my head no, "Don't be silly."

"I feel bad leaving you alone all day," she admits.

"Girl please, just because my love life has gone to shit doesn't mean yours has to suffer. I wanted you and Max to get back together forever; there's no way I'm getting in the way of that," I say.

She beams, "Yea; he told me at the party that you saw him and invited him! I definitely owe you."

The party. Knots form in my throat, and I become quiet.

Jade takes notice and is instantly apologetic, "Shit, I'm so sorry Blair."

I quietly nod and look down at the floor. She joins

me on the bed, taking a seat beside me.

"It will get easier you know."

I look at her, "When?"

I was desperate to get over the pain I was feeling.

She places her arm on my shoulder, "One day. But until then, it's perfectly fine to feel every emotion you're feeling and get it out of your system. Just take it day by day. If you want to talk or vent, you know I'm here and so is Kara."

I softly smile, "Thank you."

We hug and then she says, "Of course boo."

Once she leaves, I lie back on her bed and stare at the ceiling. I feel restless and uncomfortable. I stand up and pace the room, unsure of what to do. I walk over to the window and take a peek outside. The sun is beginning to set, casting warm rays of soft pink and sorbet orange through the sky.

Suddenly, I'm grabbing my things and rushing outside to hail a taxi. Once I find one, I hop inside and tell the driver my destination. I relax a bit and sit back in my seat, watching the city and last days of summer pass me by. After a silent fifteen-minute ride, we pull up in front, and I hand the driver a fifty-dollar bill and tell him to keep the change.

I get out and shut the door behind me. I slowly walk up the steps towards the one-bedroom condo and see that the lights are on. Once at the door, I softly knock and wait. After a moment or two, the door swings open and Jayson's eyes light up. I look at the floor and walk inside as he closes and locks the door behind me.

2

H er eyes are doll-like, big and curious. She mindlessly nibbles on her tiny knuckles; something she found to be soothing when she wasn't latched on to her mother's breast. Blair smiles, watching her with admiration. The precious baby is so beautiful and innocent with the whole world in front of her. Blair longed to be a mother and felt it was one of the best things she would do in her lifetime. All the fame and accolades for her artwork couldn't possibly compare to birthing a life. The baby looks at her and smiles, revealing her bare pink gums; she is the spitting image of her father. Blair instinctively picks her up, softly cradling her in her arms.

"Hey baby girl," she whispers.

The baby reaches up and touches her hair, cooing with joy.

"Give me my baby!"

Her voice sends chills down Blair's spine. Renee walks up and snatches the baby right out of her hands; leaving her stunned and *speechless. To Blair's horror, Renee takes her baby and walks towards a car with Jayson standing beside it. He opens the door and helps Renee inside while ignoring Blair.*

Blair cries out, "Jayson, what are you doing? I thought you wanted to be with me?"

"I want to be with my family," he declares.

He hops into the car and pulls off, leaving Blair and nothing but dust behind him.

I wake up in a cold sweat. My breathing is heavy and loud with angst. I close my eyes and try to calm my nerves. *It was only a dream. It was only a dream.*

I check the time, and it's half past one in the morning. Jayson turns over, in a peaceful slumber. The mere sight of him annoys me, and I roll my eyes. I lie onto my back and stare up at the ceiling, willing myself to fall back to sleep. But after ten minutes, I'm still very much awake and restless. I rise out of bed and reach for my silk house robe before walking over to our balcony window and peeking out into the night.

The first snowflakes of December have arrived, coating our neighborhood with frosty snow. I admire the peacefulness of it, but then I grow envious of a feeling that's so foreign to me. Since taking Jayson back, things have been interesting, to say the least. He has tried his best to make up for his mistake, and I want to believe that it was just that. However, trusting him is a struggle that I'm faced with daily. Some days are easier than others, but most are hard as hell. I still struggle with trusting him. But that's normal right? I mean, when I came back, we had a thorough discussion about our future and where it was headed. He and Renee would only converse when it concerned the baby, and that was that. I'm thankful for his commitment to getting our relationship back on track, but it's not always easy. Every now and again, there's something that sets me back. Whether it's a song on the radio, my nightmares, or when she calls. Just like that, it feels like my birthday happened only yesterday. We fight, but we always make up. If I'm being honest, the merry-go-round is driving me insane. I'm not sure how to get off, or if I truly want to.

I go downstairs and walk into the kitchen. After reaching for my favorite antique teapot, I fill it with some water and place it on top of the stove before igniting the flames. I grab my favorite mug, honey, and chamomile tea and place them on the marble counter top. While I wait, I grab my spout and water my beloved household plants.

A few moments later, the pot hisses and I quickly turn off the burner, not wanting to wake Jayson. I pour the water and take a seat on the barstool at the counter. My hands are shaky, and my mind is in shambles; I hate when I get like this. I stare into space and try to erase my nightmare from my head. Before I know it, my tea is nearly gone, and I'm still no closer to feeling relaxed.

Frustrated, I mindlessly roam the house, fixing and adjusting anything that appears to be out of place. I dust off the tribal art and gold accent pieces that decorate my living and dining rooms and put away old mail. Finally, I end up in my studio, a den that I converted into my workspace, and a place I haven't made much use of in the last couple of months. Some days, I come in here and sit for hours, willing some inspiration to pour into my soul and out onto the canvas. I try pulling from my imagination, but every time I do, I draw a blank. It's as if my soul is empty and there's no life left, no dreams. Fears that I've lost my gift consume me, making me feel depressed all over again. I quickly close the door and settle back into the living room.

Taking a seat on the couch, I turn on the TV before reaching for my hairbrush on the wooden coffee table. I brush my hair, which has been straighter than usual. In an attempt to reconcile this relationship, I want to make sure I'm everything Jayson wants. Part of the reason his cheating with Renee hurt so much is that she is painstakingly pretty. Like long hair, light skinned, light eyed pretty. Although I've never felt bad about my deep complexion, and always loved the skin I was in along with my big natural hair in all its kinky and curly glory, a part of me wonders if he was drawn to her because she was the complete opposite of who I am. So, instead of rocking my usual curls and natural tresses, I've opted for blowouts and getting it straightened every few weeks. Jayson seems to love it, often complimenting and saying how sexy my new hairdo makes me look.

I'll admit, I've done my fair share of social media stalking. Renee is a twenty-three-year-old student and a cocktail waitress by night. I assume that she and Jayson met on one of his many nights spent out with his friends while he left me at home to be alone. The thought of it all makes me sick. I can't help but wonder, what she has that I don't.

Regardless of his reason for straying, I'm committed to making things right again. I don't know how or what it's going to take. All I know is that the thought of being apart hurts tremendously more than staying together. You have to understand; Jayson and I have been together for over seven years now. He's all I know. Yes, we were young, and things got serious between us extremely fast, but it felt right, and it still does. I know that we're meant to be together. Yes, we've had our share of hiccups, and I've caught him texting other girls, but that's all. I figured his mistakes were merely growing pains. No one is perfect, right? I just want our relationship to succeed. What good is all this time and effort invested if it means nothing in the end?

I love Jayson with all my heart. Even when it hurts, even when I feel like I'm suffocating, even when I feel as if I'm drowning. I've given him the best of me, mentally, spiritually, physically, and emotionally. Who am I, if I'm not with him? We've worked so hard and built so much together, how can that all just disappear in an instant? It was a mistake. A mistake he told me, as a matter of fact, swore to me would never happen again. I am the woman he wants to be with; I am the woman he wants to spend his life with regardless of his current situation. Still, through all the hurt, pain, and betrayal I want to believe him. Lord knows I try. At this point, I have no choice but to. Because in three months, our lives will change forever.

In three months, the baby that he created with another woman will take its first breath. The thought of it still is too much to bear. Because as much as I hate him for what he's done to me, I can't stand the thought of him having a baby with another woman and living happily ever after with her. That was always supposed to be my gift to him. I should be the one birthing his first child. She stole that moment from me, and he allowed her to.

I secretly hold out hope that the baby isn't his. I even made him promise me to get a DNA test. I've tried my best to be supportive and understanding, but sometimes I feel my spirit evaporating. Each time he takes her call or attends a doctor's visit a piece of me dies. But I can't abandon him. He promised me that he would fix this and work through it, and that includes taking care of his responsibilities first. Even at the expense of my happiness.

"What kind of man would I be if I abandoned a child I fathered Blair?" he asked.

Of course, it was one of the nights she called a little too late for my comfort, and I voiced my discontent. My friends think I'm crazy and don't hold back their disapproval; but they just don't understand. They've never been in a serious relationship, not like Jayson's and mine. Yes, Jade and Max are still going strong, but they're still in that honeymoon phase that is bound to wear off. And Kara, bless her heart, doesn't have the slightest clue when it comes to getting a man to commit.

This is now my life. I don't know whether to run, scream, or have a nervous breakdown. The only thing that keeps me somewhat sane is art. Sometimes, I go to the museum and get lost for hours. But I haven't been able to create anything meaningful in months. Each time I try, it's like my psyche goes blank and inspiration goes running for the hills. I'm trying to be strong; I have to be. But I don't know how much more of this I can take.

I grab a joint and light it up. Lately, I've been smoking way more than I am accustomed to. But weed was the only thing that quieted my angst and helped me sleep for the last few months. After letting the chronic spread throughout my system, I walk back into the kitchen and place my used dishes into the sink. I hear soft footsteps on the stairs and know that Jayson is up. I'm in no mood to pretend like I'm ok, but I also don't want to start a fight simply because I woke up on the wrong side of bed.

He enters the kitchen and approaches me, "What are you doing up?"

"Bad dream," I reply.

Jayson asks, "Again?"

Desperate to avoid this conversation, I quickly nod and take another hit of my joint.

I rise onto my toes and give him a quick peck on the cheek, "I'm going back to bed."

"Alright, I'll be up in a minute," he says.

I disappear upstairs and reenter our bedroom, stripping off my robe and crawling back into bed. Once more, I try to clear my mind and relax. The moonlight creeps into the room, and I let out a loud sigh willing myself back to sleep. Suddenly, Jayson's iPhone illuminates, lighting the room up. I quickly turn my back to it and squeeze my eyes shut. Refusing to take the bait and look through his phone.

A few days later, I walk into Carver Middle School. Once a week, I teach art to a group of kids through a local community arts program that focuses on uplifting the inner city youth. It's much like one of the programs I attended as a teen. The moment I discovered it on a school flyer, I rushed home. I'll never forget begging my father to pull me out of my piano lessons and allow me to take up art. I graduated to painting when I went to college. It was one of the key moments in my life that I found my true voice. Taking those classes was just as liberating as the first time I came across one of my favorite paintings at a local flea market in Arizona. I went home and tried drawing everything that I could. More than fifteen years later, my love for art has never faltered.

After losing my dad to a car accident two years ago, I inherited a large sum of money. I've been lucky enough to live my life without worrying about working a standard nine to five. Instead, I have a substantial amount saved in the bank, and I'm able to spend my time focusing on my craft and other passions of mine. This job doesn't pay much, but it's one of the things that keep me going. What I do here has nothing to do with the money. I've always loved kids and helping them see their fullest potential meant the world to me. Being an only child, I know what it's like to feel alone and be angry but having no clue how to express those feelings. In many ways, I can see myself in a lot of these kids. I only hope that I have the same type of impact that my early art teachers had on me. I walk into class and see my students: six ambitious, rambunctious, yet amazing teens.

They see me, and their faces light up, "Hey Ms. Montgomery!" they yell in unison.

I smile, "Hey guys, how's your day going?"

"Good except for this damn snow!! Shit be drawlin!" Malik, the oldest and most outspoken says.

"Well, it's winter time! Before you know it summer will be here, and you all will be complaining about how hot it is," I joke.

The classroom laughs and I reach for my black apron before taking a seat on top of my desk.

I begin, "Ok, so what do you guys want to paint today?"

The classroom becomes quiet with high contemplation.

"What about our fantasy?" Yesenia, one of my most engaged students, says.

"Eww!" the class cries out.

Their silliness amuses me.

"Shh!" I order before making my way around the classroom. "I like that Yesenia, but why don't we expand on it a bit. How about we paint our idea of the perfect place? Somewhere that you've actually been to, always wanted to go to, or imagined."

My students seem enthused and eagerly get to work.

I reach for my iPad and connect it to my Bluetooth speaker, turning on some Lauryn Hill tunes. After a few minutes, I walk around, giving pointers and reassurance to my students and their creations.

By the end of class, my mood has improved drastically. I swear these kids are my saving grace; being with them always makes everything better, even if it's only for an hour or so.

I pack up my bag and pull out my phone. I have a few notifications and immediately check them. Once I respond to all of them, I decide to check my Instagram and catch up on the latest posts from the day. I see that Jayson posted a selfie of himself at work. Naturally, I check the comments to see the responses. After a moment I quickly exit out and put my phone down. *So much for my good mood.* I put my phone back into my bag and head home.

When I arrive, Jayson is seated comfortably on the couch watching television. I ignore him, removing my parka coat and snow boots before walking into the kitchen.

"Well hello," he comes in after me,

I waste no time, "Who is Dimepiece87?"

"What?"

"You two seemed to be real friendly on your post today," I observe.

Jayson shakes his head, "Blair, its only Instagram. I can't help what those girls say to me on there. Besides, it's a pic, not real life. We're real; our relationship is real, so stop sweating dumb shit."

I refuse to back down, "You can't control what they say, but you can control what you entertain Jayson. Why do any of those girls feel it's even appropriate to say those types of things to you? Don't they know you have a girlfriend?"

Jayson sighs and shakes his head again, "Of course they know, I'm not hiding anything. I can't believe we are having another fight about this!"

"Well it will continue to be a problem until I see differently," I say.

"Whatever man."

I instantly roll my eyes. I was sick to death of having this conversation and feeling this way. I love Jayson with all my heart, but sometimes I feel he values the attention he gets from his damn phone more than he does our relationship.

3

The next day, I pull into the retirement community and smoothly park my silver Volvo in the designated visitor's space. After turning my car off, I hop out and hurry towards the front entrance. I punch the access code into the keypad and wait for the sliding doors to open. Once inside, I make my way towards the elevator and get on. I check my watch, pleased that I'm on time, and push five for my destination. A few minutes later, I use my spare key to enter my grandmother's apartment and am instantaneously greeted by the smell of cinnamon rolls.

"Blair is that you?" she calls out to me from the bathroom.

"Yes mam," I say as I enter the kitchen and cut into the sweet confection she just baked.

Just as I take a bite, Gran is standing in the entryway rubbing lotion into her delicate hands.

"So you just gon' come into my house and eat my food without giving me a proper hello?" she charges.

I smile and kiss her on the cheek.

"Hey Gran," I say.

Gran is my world, my rock, and my calm between the many storms in my life. Without her, I don't know who or where I'd be. She's the one thing in my life that gives me stability, especially during my dark times in my past. Being an only child of a short-lived marriage, I struggled with feeling like I belonged. My parents tried their best to give me a two-parent household, but they ended up at each other's throats in the end. As a result, my mother picked me up and moved across the country to start over. I was miserable, and my mother knew it. After nearly a year and a new boyfriend, we decided as a family that I'd be better suited if I stayed with my father. Truly, it was the best thing for me. Although I was my father's princess and he gave me the world, he worked a lot. So I spent many days and nights with my Gran. She knew about my cutting, having discovered healing scars when I first moved back. Gran patched me up and kept me in line, teaching me other ways to deal with any stress or any disappointment I faced. We needed each other, with my father being an only child himself, I was her only grandchild, and we were close. When he passed away, it was one of the hardest things we were forced to deal with together. She has always been there for me, and I was there for her.

Her face lights up, "Hey baby. How's my favorite girl doing?"

I shrug, "I'm hanging in there. How are you feeling?"

"You know me, blessed as always," she says.

"You ready to go?" I ask.

She rolls her eyes and nods her head as I help her into her favorite down coat. Back outside, I guide her into my car before jumping into the driver's seat and pulling off to make it to her medical appointment. The winter cold still lingers in the car, so I reach over and adjust the car's heat. Gran tugs on her hat, pulling it over her short curly grey hair.

"Have you talked to your mother lately?" she asks.

I nod, "Yes, she's good. Living in Brazil now."

"That woman sure stays on the move," Gran snickers.

My mother lives a Bohemian lifestyle. She's always been unconventional with the way she viewed life. While she wanted to be free and explore the universe (as she calls it) my father wanted to be comfortable, settle down and take care of his family. Once a dancer, living such a monotone life made her miserable. If I'm being honest, my father never stood a chance. I don't blame him one bit for being enamored with my mother; she's truly one of a kind. While he never remarried, men continued to worship my mom, and she loved them and left them as she saw fit. Jade always admired her, especially because she adopted that same mentality in college. (That has since changed since she met Max of course.) My mother, on the other hand, hasn't changed one bit. She now travels at her leisure and is currently on husband number four. I see her at least once a year and talk to her often, but Gran definitely fills the void of my mother being so far away.

"So how's Jayson?" Gran asks, interrupting my thoughts.

I coolly answer, "He's fine."

She isn't buying it, "Really? It doesn't seem fine. You know I can tell when you're lying. I can see it all on your face."

Gran is right, I've never been good at hiding my true feelings from her, she could see right through me.

I sigh, "Some days are good, but a lot are bad. I want to believe he's changed, but it's so hard," I finally admit.

I didn't tell her every detail concerning our relationship, but she knew that we were having problems. She was particularly concerned because I was losing weight and vanishing into thin air, as she calls it. Besides all of that, she's never judged me.

"Be sure to pray on it," she instructs. "If he's the right man for you, God will show you. And if he's not, the truth will slap you right in the face."

I chuckle at her logic and park in the free space next to the doctor's office. Inside, Gran is swiftly checked in and seen after only a couple of minutes. Once we make it back to the examination room, her physician Dr. Amhad enters.

He greets her with a warm smile, "Hello Ms. Loretta! How are you?"

"I'm hanging in there," she smiles.

Dr. Amhad performs his usual routine, checking her vitals and blood pressure, writing notes and asking her questions regarding her current state.

"Alright Ms. Loretta, your blood pressure is very high, we are going to have to work to get that down. Please be mindful of the foods you are eating, which means no more Dr. Pepper."

One thing my grandmother loved was Dr. Pepper. I even love it because that's all she had in her fridge when I was a kid. The problem is, she hasn't cut back on her intake no matter how much her doctor or I lecture. She hates being told what to do, what she can't eat, and how many meds she needs to be taking. She's very old school, and when her mind is made up, there is little you can do to get her to change it.

By the end of the appointment, Gran is ready to get out of there. She rises from the examination bed and puts on her coat. After Dr. Ahmad excuses himself, I softly take her hand.

"Gran, I love you, but you've got to start listening to the doctor's orders and cut back on the salt and sugar. You need to be drinking more water," I plead.

She dismissively nods, "I'll try."

In an attempt to cheer her up, I treat her to lunch and a trip to the local bookstore. By the end of our day together, she's back to her normal chipper self with a bunch of new magazines to read.

"Please make sure you're taking care of yourself ok?" I say as I help her out of her coat.

She gently pats me on the back, "I will baby. Don't

go worrying yourself about me."

I turn on the television while she takes a seat in her favorite chair.

"I love you, I'll see you next week," I say, before leaning down and planting a kiss on her cheek.

"Love you too."

With Christmas fast approaching, Jade, Kara and I meet up for brunch and spend the rest of the afternoon braving the winter cold and holiday crowds. After hours of standing in line and exploring Center City in search of the perfect gifts for our loved ones, we settle into a charming coffee shop to get lattes and warm up. I take a sip of my white mocha drink and tug on my favorite wool scarf as we make our way back outside. It's now five o'clock, the sun had set, and the winds are sharp and ice cold. The day was fun yet exhausting, and we were all ready to go home.

"So what are we doing for New Year's?" Jade asks.

I shrug, "I'm not really in the mood to go out, to be honest."

My friends roll their eyes at my objection. To say the least, I haven't been in the mood to do much of anything over the last couple of months. That didn't stop them from inviting me everywhere or constantly nagging me about neglecting my social life.

Jade throws her arm around my shoulders, "Stop being such a Grinch!"

Kara giggles as a mob of children and their parents rush past us crossing the street.

"Aw look at all the little kiddies," Kara says.

I feel myself cringe. Yes, I love kids, but seeing babies and toddlers makes my stomach turn. Quite honestly, when I see one, I try my best to keep my distance.

Kara observes, "Oh! They're about to start the light show."

"Let's go check it out, I haven't been down to see it in a while," Jade says.

"Do we have to?" I whine.

Kara and Jade look at me, both sick of my negativity. I roll my eyes before taking another sip of my latte and looking at the ground. Before I can voice another protest, my friends drag me across the street to Franklin Square.

Each holiday season the park is transformed into a winter wonderland that people congregate to in droves. Thousands of jewel-colored lights dance on the trees with all the holiday classics playing in the background. If you aren't in the Christmas spirit, five minutes in this place will change that. Normally, I'd be all for it, but I really wasn't in the mood.

Inside, everyone is all smiles. Small children enjoy the carousel rides while teens and happy couples play miniature golf. Vendors are lined up selling holiday treats including cookies, cakes, and winter beers. Families, small and large, tote holiday shopping bags as their dogs navigate the busy pathways anticipating the next show. After a few moments, "Jingle Bells" starts playing and red, green, gold, blue and white lights shine, lighting up the trees and night sky.

Once the show ends, we make our way out of the park and towards the garage to retrieve our cars. To my surprise, I enjoyed myself. It felt good to be distracted from the chaos in my life, even if it was only for a few moments.

"That was fun," I admit.

Jade seems pleased, "See!"

"Yes, I love this time of year!" Kara agrees.

My friends gloat as we wait for our chance to cross the street. Traffic is as busy as ever. Cars are piled onto the narrow streets, eager to reach their destinations. While we wait for the light to change, I look up and notice a familiar face.

I squint, "Mrs. Adams?"

She looks exactly the same, curvy, with deep bronze skin and a bald head. A few years older, but time is definitely on her side. As soon as she realizes who I am, her eyes light up with joy.

She beams, "Oh my goodness, Blair! How are you doing?"

We share a warm hug.

"It's so great to see you! Happy holidays," I say, trying to sound as pleasant as I can be.

Mrs. Adams was one of my favorite professors back at Temple. She's a quirky woman and highly artistic. I can credit her with helping me realize my true talent as an artist. I always admired her spirit and how she has the ability to light up an entire room with her presence. In a way, you can say I looked up to her. She had the life I always wanted: her passion, art, her man, and a job she loved.

"Same to you!" she smiles and looks to my friends, "Getting that holiday shopping done?"

We all nod.

I say, "These are my friends, Kara and Jade. Ladies this is Mrs. Adams, one of my favorite art teachers!"

"Call me Grace," she glows.

They give her a warm greeting, exchanging hugs like they've known one another for years.

"It was so great seeing you, Blair, we have to stay in touch!" she says.

I eagerly nod, "I'd love that."

"Why don't you ladies come to my New Year's Eve party? That's if you don't have plans of course. It's a black-tie affair, and I would just love to have some young beauties in the mix to shake things up," she says.

A night of drinks, parties, and glam. I knew my friends would kill me if I declined.

"Yes, we'd love to!" I reply.

"Can we bring dates?" Jade asks.

"Of course," Mrs. Adams says.

Kara can't hide her excitement, "Oh that sounds wonderful! Now I have to find the perfect dress."

Mrs. Adams smiles and nods, "Yes, it's going to be a great time."

She reaches into her purse and pulls out a glossy black business card with gold script before handing it to me.

"Here's my contact info, be sure to email me so that I can send you all the details," she instructs.

I nod before placing it into my coat pocket, "It was so good seeing you."

We hug once more before parting ways.

Kara says, "That was so dope!"

Jade agrees, "Yes! I can't wait."

I remain silent as we cross the street.

"Blair, you better email her for that party information!" Jade scolds.

"I will," I say.

After saying goodbye to my friends, I hop into my car feeling more upbeat than I had in months. Seeing Mrs. Adams was a breath of fresh air, and I realize how much I miss the person I was when I am attending her classes. Back then, I had a hunger; I was so driven. I missed that, and I was determined to get it back.

She takes a sip of her drink and bops to the music. College was officially over, and she was anxious to start this new chapter in her life. The time had come for her to see the world, and go after her dreams finally. Her eyes quickly scan the room for her best friend and accomplice for the evening. After a moment she spots her friend in the corner flirting with one of her many admirers. She silently chuckles to herself and takes another sip of her drink, a concoction of cheap liquor and fruit punch. It was the last party of the year, and she planned to enjoy it to the fullest. Unfortunately for her, she had one too many drinks and an extreme urge to pee. On her way to

the bathroom, she bumps into Luis, the school's star basketball point-guard and legendary heartbreaker.

"Can I talk to you real quick?" he asks.

She softly smiles; the last thing she wanted to do was talk, but she had one person in front of her for the bathroom. After a slight moment of contemplation, she nods. He smiles before taking a place beside her in the tight frat-house corridor.

Luis cracks a smile, "You look really nice tonight."

She smiles before softly adjusting her short denim skirt and tank top, "Thank you. So what's up?"

The bathroom door swings open and three drunk and chatty girls rush out. She sighs with relief, only a few more moments before she can ditch Luis. As he talks, she wants to tune him out; she really had no interest in being another one of his conquests. For some reason, he's not his usual calm, overly arrogant self. In fact, he seems to be a bit frustrated, anxious even. Suddenly, Luis pushes up on her, taking her completely by surprise. He grabs her wrist much more aggressively than she would have liked.

"You're hurting me, Luis," she complains.

Her eyes dart up and down the hallway in search of help. She's terrified when she realizes that no one takes notice. Her heart races as she presses her back up against the cold wall.

"What are you doing? Stop!" she chokes.

He ignores her pleads and tries kissing her. Panic takes over as she tries to dodge his drunken advances.

She screams out, "Stop it!"

"Just relax, I know you want me," he whispers.

Now she was getting angry. Using all of her might, she tries to push him away. However, he doesn't budge. She balls up her fists, but before she can do damage, a soft hand grabs hers.

"Hey babe, sorry I'm so late," he says with confidence. He then looks at Luis, "We got a problem here?"

She quickly turns around to see an unfamiliar face. Almost instantly, his keen, almond-brown eyes take her aback. He's slim and significantly taller than her. His dark brown hair is cut low complimenting his butterscotch skin.

Luis instantly backs down, "Nah, we're good. I didn't know she was spoken for."

Without saying another word, he cowers away and walks back into the party as if nothing happened.

"Are you alright?" Superman asks.

She quickly blinks and nods her head, "Thank you."

He nods, "Don't mention it."

The bathroom door swings open, but she barely notices. Butterflies take over the fear that once invaded her body. She nervously looks at the floor and tucks her curly hair behind her right ear.

He asks, "So what's your name?"

"Blair."

Superman smiles, "It's nice to meet you, Blair, I'm Jayson."

I wake up, and it's Christmas morning. I sit up and rub the sleep out of my eyes. Memories of the night I met Jayson still linger in my mind. That was the day I always said my life changed for the better, but lately I'm not so sure. I pull myself out of bed; walk into the bathroom and splash water on my face before brushing my teeth. I can smell bacon frying as I make my way down the stairs. I enter the kitchen and see Jayson making pancakes. Once he hears me come in, he turns around and smiles.

"Good Morning," he says.

"Morning," I reply.

This last week has been rather peaceful. Jayson has been very attentive, affectionate, and most of all loving. Maybe it's the holidays, or maybe he finally has changed for the better. I felt hope, and it feels good.

He flips a pancake onto an empty plate; they're blueberry, my favorite. I take a seat at the counter. I can't tell you the last time this man cooked, let alone cooked for me. *Oh yea, my birthday.* The memory makes my stomach squirm.

I watch him with caution, "What's all this?"

"Can't I make the love of my life a little breakfast?" he smiles.

"Ok," unsure of where this was going. "Thank you," I add.

He is acting strange, high-strung and fidgeting around. Finally, he sets a plate down in front of me containing blueberry pancakes, cheese eggs, and bacon, burnt and crispy just how I like it. He then fixes his own plate and takes a seat beside me. I remain silent and cut into my food.

After a moment he says, "I'm thirsty, can you grab the orange juice?"

"Seriously?"

He nods. Not in the mood to start a fight, I get up and make my way over to the fridge. I open it and lean down to grab the OJ before turning around. To my surprise, he's in front of me kneeling down on one knee, his eyes nervous. In his hand, he's holding a three-carat diamond ring.

"What is that?" I ask.

"A promise," he says.

Now I'm really annoyed, "You got me a motherfucking promise ring?"

He ignores me, "Blair, you're the best thing that has happened to me. I know I messed up and hurt you, but I promise to be a better man for you. Spend the rest of your life with me, be my wife."

I stare at him; my tongue feels like it's twisted in my throat. I've wanted this for so long, but this felt…weird. Jayson has always weird about marriage. Growing up, Jayson had the perfect family. A son of two lawyers, he and his older brother never wanted for a thing. That all changed when his mother decided to leave their father for another man, breaking up their happy home. Deep down, I know that he always resented her for it. Whenever we talked about marriage, he'd become tense and change the subject. His commitment issues were obvious, but I always figured that they would change when he realized that I was in this relationship for the long haul. I guess me almost leaving him shook him to his core enough to take a leap of faith. I stare at him and the future I've always desired at a complete loss for words. *Maybe he really has changed.* I slowly nod my head yes.

4

My body trembles and I feel like I'm flying.

"I love you so much," Jayson moans.

He's breathing heavily and a light sweat coats his forehead. After a moment, he lifts himself from between my legs and lies on his back trying to catch his breath. I smile and pull the sheets over my nude body.

I roll over to face him, "I love you too."

It's been a week since we got engaged and I feel like I'm flying. These are the moments that keep me going. Yes, our relationship has its rough patches, and we had our problems. But I can't shake the love I feel for this man. It's like a high that I don't ever want to end. He returns a smile and sits up, leaning in to give me a tender kiss on the lips.

He strokes my hair, "This is going to be a good year

for us; I can feel it."

"Me too," I smile.

"So are you ready to tell your friends? You know their nosey asses are going to notice that new rock on your finger," he teases.

I hold my left hand up, admiring the sparkle of my beautiful platinum ring.

I nod, "Yes."

"They'll probably try and talk you out of it," he snorts.

I giggle, "They wouldn't do that."

Jayson shrugs, "If you say so."

Since my birthday, Jayson has avoided all occasions where he'd have to interact with my best friends. Sadly for him, that would all change tonight. Tonight was New Year's Eve, and we'd all be bringing in the New Year together at Mrs. Adams extravagant party. After dealing with the constant badgering from Jade, I finally reached out to her as she suggested. Frankly, the thought of it all made my head spin.

I sit up, "I need to get up, or I'm going to miss my hair appointment."

Jayson quickly throws his arms around me in a bear hug.

"Five more minutes," he begs.

He gives me his best puppy dog eyes, and I can't resist.

Thirty minutes later, I step out of the shower and wrap a towel around my damp body. After drying off, I grab my favorite body cream and delicately rub it into my skin. As I approach our bedroom, I hear Jayson on the phone.

"Yes, I'll be free to meet this week," he states.

I pause for a moment, listening for more; my heart is pounding through my chest. I struggle to catch my breath as he hangs up and gets out of the bed. Determined to remain casual, I enter the bedroom and head straight for my underwear drawer. Moments later he approaches me, pressing up against my naked back. Part of me wants to push him away, and question who was on the phone, but I refuse to ruin our great morning, or week, for that matter. We've been doing so well, and I felt guilty for tarnishing it. He leans in, kissing the back of my neck and wrapping his arms around my body.

"I have some good news," he whispers into my ear.

"Oh, yea? What's that?" I say, trying to be nonchalant.

"That was my boss Whitney, she wants to meet this week to discuss me leading the new Taylor account," he boasts.

I quickly turn around, "Oh my god! That's great babe!"

I pull him in for a tight hug, throwing my arms around his shoulders.

"I still can't believe she called," he says.

I cheer, "I'm sure you'll do great!"

He blushes, "I hope so; this could take my career to the next level."

Jayson works at a small web development firm in addition to doing some freelance work on the side. He always wanted to own his own company one day, and I truly believe that he has the ability to do so. He's one of the smartest people I know, and it's one of the things that I love most about him. I dress in a hurry and kiss him before I rush out the door to my hair appointment.

I slide on my gown and admire what I see. It's a long silhouette with long sleeves and an open back. The vibrant shade of emerald green compliments my skin, and when I saw it at Bloomingdale's, I thought it was perfect for the formal affair. I unhook the last of the pins in my hair and fluff out my large curls. My hair is elegant, yet voluminous, falling past my shoulders. I was thankful to my hair stylist for her great work. I can hear the faint sound of Jayson coming upstairs as I delicately put my ruby red lipstick on. I walk over to my dresser in search of my favorite gold bracelet that compliments the gold earrings I'm wearing. Once I find it, I look to Jayson. I can tell he's been watching me and it sends butterflies throughout my stomach. He looks like a million bucks in his tailored black suit and bow tie.

I ask, "Can you help me put this on?"

He smiles, and walks over to assist me.

Once he finishes, he says, "I really love your hair like that."

"Thank you," I blush.

I adjust my ring before reaching for my black YSL clutch. After putting on our coats, he reaches for my hand, and we exit the house on our way to the party. We pull up to the Sofitel and are instantly greeted by pleasant staff. A valet attendant grabs the keys to Jayson's black Infinity sedan, and a doorman directs us inside before showing us to the ballroom and taking our coats. Inside, the room is full of music, laughter and light conversation. Philly's elite is definitely in attendance. I walk the room, hand in hand with Jayson. Moments later, I spot my friends and approach them.

As soon as we greet them, I sense the tension. To my pleasant surprise, they all do their best to play nice. Jade is there with Max, and they look phenomenal together. She looks like a trophy, wearing a gold wrap gown with a high slit showcasing her killer legs. While Max dons a wine-colored suit jacket coupled with a crisp white shirt, black bow tie, and black tuxedo pants. I smile because they complement each other so well. Kara is vibrant in a deep plunging, floor-length royal blue gown; her hair is bone straight with new hazelnut highlights.

"I love your hair!" I compliment.

Kara blushes, "Thank you."

I ask, "Where's your date?"

I was confused because she made sure to tell me to get her a plus one only a few days ago.

"He's getting drinks. It's only my brother girl," she explains.

"Oh, Kai's back in town?"

She nods, "Yea he just moved back."

Suddenly Jade's eyes grow big, "Hold up!" She quickly reaches over and grabs my hand, "What's that on your finger?"

Kara grips my hand next, examining my ring. Her jaw drops and my face flushes.

I take a deep breath, "Jayson and I are getting married."

My friends stare at me completely dumbfounded as I timidly weave my fingers into his. Everyone remains silent, clearly trying to process the nuclear bomb I just dropped on them. I still can't believe it myself, especially after what he's put me through. I swear you could hear a pin drop.

Finally, Max says, "Congrats to you both."

He gives Jayson a handshake and me a hug. Kara soon follows, throwing her arms around me.

"Congratulations," she says.

But I swear it sounds more like a question than a well wish. Jade reluctantly follows suit, her eyes filled with sadness. I try my best to avoid them.

"Congratulations," she whispers before hugging me.

Jayson excuses himself to go to the bathroom and to grab us some drinks, leaving me to face the interrogation of my friends. But luckily for me, a familiar face approaches us and hands Kara a glass of champagne. He looks different; more muscular than I remember. As soon as he sees me, his eyes light up.

"What's up Blair?" Kai smiles, smooth as ever.

I give him a warm hug, "Hey Kai! It's been a minute."

He looks handsome in his dark grey tailored suit and tie. His hair is cut low showing a sea of waves on his head, and his face is clean-shaven and smooth. Standing at about six foot four, it wasn't hard for him to stand out in a crowd.

By now, Jayson returns with drinks, and I introduce them both. Just then, Mrs. Adams approaches with her husband, Braxton. She looks regal in her black lace ball gown. I don't think I've ever seen her look so beautiful.

"You all look phenomenal! So glad that you are here," she gloats. She turns to Mr. Adams, an older Caucasian man, "Honey, these are those darling girls I was telling you about. Blair is one of my favorite art students."

Mr. Adams smiles and gives us all a sincere greeting, "Hello, it's a pleasure to meet you all."

"Thanks again for inviting us." I smile, "This is Max, Kai, and my fiancé Jayson."

Mrs. Adams beams, "Fiancé? Oh my goodness, congratulations are in order!"

She warmly greets Jayson and the rest of the fellas. After a few moments of small talk, one of the staff members approaches the married couple and whispers into Mr. Adams' ear.

He turns towards the group, "Please excuse us, the countdown is going to begin shortly."

Then he whisks his wife away. The two take the center of the stage in front of the DJ booth.

"Thank you, everyone, for attending our annual gala and for bringing in the New Year with my beautiful wife and I. You all look sensational if I do say so myself," Mr. Adams says through the microphone. He continues,

"There are waiters walking around with champagne, if you don't have a glass, please take one. The countdown is about to start."

Everyone in the crowd obliges, excited to drink and toast to the night. A few minutes later, we are all counting down to the future ahead.

"Three, two, one! Happy New Year!" the crowd cheers.

I turn to my fiancé and kiss him tenderly on his lips. Hopeful for the new chapter in our lives. The DJ picks things up, playing the most popular songs from the past year. The rest of the night goes on without a hitch. We continue to eat, drink, and party like there is no tomorrow. By the end of the night, I'm exhausted and ready to go home. I catch up with Mrs. Adams, who's still busy working the crowd.

"Blair! What a night!" she says greeting me with a hug.

"Yes, we had such a great time! Thank you for having us," I say.

She replies, "Of course honey. But before you leave, you have to meet my closest friend. She's amazing, and I couldn't stop telling her about you!"

Before I can object, she's pulling me through the crowd to the bar to meet Angelique Graves, a well-known philanthropist. I knew because I followed her work, setting up schools in impoverished countries and helping the less fortunate. This woman was a big fucking deal, and way prettier in person. She's about my height and fair skinned with freckles. Her honey-colored dreadlocks are pulled into a high bun.

"Angie! This is Blair, the wonderful artist that I was telling you about!" Mrs. Adams brags.

Angelique greets me with a smile and hug, "It's so nice to meet you finally, Blair, I've heard a lot of great things about you."

I'm truly flattered, "Wow, I can't believe it. It's lovely to meet you. I'm a big fan of your work. Being able to travel the world and help others has always been a dream of mine."

Angelique remains gracious, "Traveling is good for the soul! Where have you been so far?"

I become nervous, "Oh, only to Paris a few years back to visit my mother."

Mrs. Adams throws her arm around my shoulder interrupting us, "Angie, tell her!"

She's clearly drunk but seeing her act this way is amusing.

Angie giggles at her friend and turns her attention back to me, "Well, Grace was telling me that you're an artist and about your passion for teaching underprivileged children in the community."

I nod, "Yes, I love it."

"I'm setting up a new program in India this spring, with a focus on the arts. How would you feel about teaching with us?"

"India?" I ask.

She nods her head, "Only for a few months. But food, lodging, supplies, all of that will be taken care of. Do you have a passport?"

I can't hide my excitement. This was something I've always wanted to do.

"Yes, yes I do!" I answer.

"Perfect. My team could use someone like you," she says.

I answer, "That sounds amazing, I don't know what to say."

"You don't have to give me a definite answer right now. How about you take my business card and think it over," Angelique offers.

"I'd love that," I smile.

She then reaches into her purse and hands me one. I give her and Mrs. Adams a hug before I rejoin Jayson and my friends who are all ready to call it a night. We all walk towards the exit and retrieve our coats and then cars from the valet. I hug all my friends goodbye once our car is pulled up. On the way home I'm ecstatic. I immediately tell Jayson about my introduction to Angelique and the amazing opportunity she offered. He stays silent nodding his head and listening while driving.

"What did you tell her?" he asks.

"I didn't give her an answer yet, but I definitely want to do it. I've wanted to go to India since I was a little girl. So to be there and be able to teach is a dream come true!" I boast.

"Well you can't do that," he firmly states.

I'm suddenly confused, "What do you mean I can't do that?"

Jayson keeps his eyes on the road, but I can see the tension in his jaw. He's upset, and I can't understand why.

Shouldn't he be happy for me?

He asks, "You think it's ok to go to another continent while you're engaged to be married?"

"What's the big deal? It's only for a couple of months," I say.

"What's wrong with your teaching job here? What do you think teaching a bunch of poor ass kids across the world is going to do? You can't save everyone," he pauses. "You don't do things like that when you're in a relationship, or especially when you're someone's fiancé. You should be home with me," he affirms.

"Why are you making it seem like I have to choose?" I question.

He coolly replies, "Because you do."

I argue, "So it's ok for you to chase your dreams but I can't pursue my own?"

He shakes his head, "My dreams aren't taking me halfway around the world. How can I take this relationship seriously if you're so willing to give up on what we have and leave?"

I can't believe my ears. The fact that he refuses to support something I've always dreamed about hurts more than the cheating ever could. I bite my bottom lip and fight back my tears.

"That's really selfish Jayson," I protest.

Jayson quickly shakes his head, "No it's not. How does that look? We're engaged, and you move to India."

I cross my arms, "I don't know. How does it look being engaged while you have a baby on the way with another woman?"

He sucks his teeth, "It's not the same thing."

"No, it's not even close," I murmur.

5

few weeks later, I place my overnight bag in the trunk and hop into Jade's car. Today is Kara's thirtieth birthday, and she wanted nothing more than to be low-key this year. So instead of our usual lavish turn-up, she decided to have a slumber party. Jade and I were ordered to bring our best pajamas and be ready to have a good time.

We head over to Kara's new apartment located in the outskirts of Philly. The area is up and coming, the rumored new hot spot for young professionals. After parking, we grab our things and enter the newly constructed and obviously expensive apartment building.

The door to her apartment is unlocked, and we let ourselves into her place. This was my first time there since she moved and boy was I amazed. It's modern and white with a futuristic feel to it. The ceilings are high, and the floors are glossy. My depression kept me from helping her move in two months ago, and I can't hide my guilt for being such a shitty friend; especially after all she's done for me. Luckily for me, Kara is one of the sweetest people on the planet, and she is always completely understanding. Once we're settled inside, she greets us wearing a white silk teddy, matching robe and furry slippers.

"Happy birthday and congratulations on your new spot," I say, handing her a gift card to her favorite home furnishing store.

Kara can't mask her excitement, "JD's! Thank you, you know I love that place."

I laugh, "Yes that's why it was so easy to get."

We share a hug, and she quickly orders us to change. Jade and I do as we're told, going into her bedroom and master bathroom to remove our clothes and swap them for our pajamas. Jade is wearing a black satin baby doll slip while I'm wearing my pink silk camisole and short set. We walk into the living room and Kara's directing four other women in matching white coats and pants. Behind them, I see three pedicure stations set up.

"Damn Kara! This is dope!" Jade praises.

When Kara sees us, her eyes light up, "Oh my god! You guys look so cute!"

Right then, the women greet us with smiles while one hands us glasses of champagne.

Kara announces, "Let my birthday festivities begin!"

We toast and take our seats. The workers instantly

get to work on our feet while the young waitress is pleasant and equally attentive, refilling our glasses whenever they're low and offering us strawberries along with other decadent treats at our leisure. I close my eyes and lie back in pure bliss. It wasn't long before we all are really tipsy, listening to Kara give a detailed account of her latest dating nightmare.

"So we've been talking for a couple days right, texting and getting to know each other. Then one day I wake up to a text from him, and it's a motherfucking dick pic!" she explains.

"Eww!" Jade and I squeal.

Kara continues, "A fucking dick picture to start my day. I had an early meeting, and that was the last thing I needed to see. So I text him like what's this? And this idiot had the nerve to reply 'You're welcome.'"

"Like he was doing you a favor by sending his stank ass penis through the mail!" I can't believe my ears.

Jade shakes her head in disbelief, "Yuck! What the fuck is wrong with these guys? Why do they think we like that shit?"

"I blocked him and haven't talked to him since," Kara shrugs.

I laugh, "I don't blame you."

"But no seriously, I'm on strike from all men for a while! They are all creeps," Kara vents.

I snort, "Yea right."

"For real, I've officially given up on dating! I need a damn break," Kara says. "I just want to focus on myself and get my mind right. I've let guys distract me for far too long."

"I hear that girl," Jade says.

"I'm so sick of giving my all to a guy and getting nothing in return or being stuck with weirdos. So fuck them all. This year is all about Kara!" she declares.

I raise my glass, "I'll toast to that!"

Kara continues, "But really though, men ain't shit."

We tap our glasses and take a sip.

"Hey, not all men are bad!" Jade interjects.

"I guess that means you and Max and getting along fine," I say, changing the subject.

Jade instantly blushes and nods, "Things are going so good. We're together like every day, and I'm not bothered by it at all. You guys know that I get bored extremely fast. But he's so supportive and loving; I love that he's not threatened by me or my ambitions. It's scary, but I'm determined not to over think and just enjoy things. You know how I can be."

"Oh, we know bitch!" Kara and I say in unison.

We burst out laughing once more.

Suddenly Kara's phone rings and she grabs it.

"Hold on guys, this is my boss," she says before stepping into the kitchen to answer.

Kara works in the banking industry. Her firm is one of the largest banks in the northeastern region and her career has been highly successful. Being only one of five other women at the corporate office, she has been making quite the name for herself since joining the company over two years ago.

A few moments later, she returns looking flushed.

Jade sits up, "What is it?"

"Yea, what's wrong?" I add.

"You're looking at the new business development lead at Majestic Bank!" Kara announces.

"Yes!" we cheer.

We hop out of our seats to hug and congratulate her. This is a major accomplishment, and I'm so excited for my friend. It seems that everyone around me is getting everything they ever wanted. We all return our seats and allow our nail technicians to finish up on our toes.

Kara is still beside herself, "Look at the universe. I swear off men and get a promotion!"

"You deserve it girl," I say.

We all raise our glasses once more and share a toast. The workers are clearly amused by her revelation but stay silent. Once they leave, Kara turns on some music, and we order takeout from her favorite Thai restaurant. After it arrives, we gather on her large black velvet sectional and proceed to stuff our faces.

Kara takes a bite of her shrimp wonton and turns to me, "Well, we know Jade is all in love and shit, and I just got a promotion, so what's new with you Blair?"

I nearly choke on my chicken Pad Thai, "Nothing."

"Girl, you're engaged, that doesn't sound like nothing to me! How does it feel?" Kara pries.

I shrug, "It feels the same I guess."

Since my birthday, it was no secret that my friends were not fond of Jayson. In fact, I remember quite clearly everything they had to say about him and our relationship. But since they found out about the engagement I could tell that they've been waiting for an explanation. I know that they are still shocked; shit so am I. But I feel like I don't owe them one. It's my life at the end of the day, and I only hope that they will continue to be supportive.

Jade can tell that I wasn't going to offer many details, so she opts to change the subject, "When do you leave for India?"

I told her about my meeting with Angelique Graves and the amazing opportunity I'd been given last week at the New Year's Eve party.

"Oh," I pause. "I'm not going."

My friends become silent, and I swear I can cut the tension with a knife.

Jade looks upset; "So you mean to tell me you're perfectly fine with marrying a man that has a baby on the way? What, are you two about to become sister-wives or some shit?"

"We don't know if it's his," I retort.

She sits up, refusing to back down, "And what if it is? What are you prepared to do?"

"You just don't understand," I say.

"Lately that's been your answer for everything," Jade dismisses.

I roll my eyes and take a sip of my champagne. Kara stays silent, eating her food. She knew to stay out of our disagreements.

Jade persists, "Seriously Blair, what are you doing?"

I look at Jade, and I swear I've never seen her look more disappointed. I quickly shrug it off and run my fingers through my hair and massage my scalp.

She continues, "Don't you realize that you're going to have to deal with that trick for the rest of your life if you marry him?"

The thought of it makes my stomach turn. But I refuse to be caught up in things that weren't facts just yet.

"I've been with the man for eight years, I can't just throw that away," I argue.

"What the hell is a relationship, or better yet, marriage with no trust?" Jade challenges.

She isn't empathetic at all.

I shrug once more, "We're working on it."

Jade yells, "But he didn't even have the decency to tell you he cheated in the first place! That bastard let you find out on your fucking birthday!"

"People do make mistakes," Kara reasons.

"Kara, you and I both know he only proposed to Blair to keep her exactly where he wants her. Shit, he's a jerk, but he isn't dumb," Jade says.

What the fuck? Her words hurt.

I argue, "How can you say that?"

Jade lectures, "Because someone has to. You really think if that girl weren't pregnant he'd stop dealing with her on his own?"

I nod, "I have to believe it."

Jade counters, "Says who?"

"Look I'm thirty years old. I've been with Jayson since I was twenty-two, what do I look like starting over?" I question.

She could see that I was a lost cause.

"If you say so," Jade shrugs.

It seems that she had finally thrown in the towel on the whole thing. *Thank goodness.*

Then Kara says, "Wait what? Women do that shit every day! For real Blair, are you delusional or just in denial?"

I was shocked that this was coming from her. I expected Jade to give me shit, but not Kara.

"What?"

She continues, "Do you hear yourself? Are you that afraid of being alone?"

I stay silent.

"It's ok if you are. I get it, but isn't your happiness more important than some guy?" Kara asks.

She has some damn nerve.

I argue, "Jayson isn't just some guy."

"And of all the guys out there, you chose to be dumb for that one. You were a person before you met him you know," Jade murmurs.

"What are you saying?" I say, turning to her.

Jade explains, "Jayson is sucking you dry, and you seem to be oblivious to it. You know damn well the reason you're not going to India is because Jayson doesn't want you to." She continues, "I've known you forever, going overseas is one of your lifelong dreams. You mean to tell me you're going to let this once in a lifetime opportunity pass you by because of that sorry excuse of a boyfriend? I'm sorry, but I've stayed silent for far too long. That man is playing you for a damn fool, and it's like you don't even care!"

I shake my head in denial, "You don't understand."

"What don't I understand? Please help me," Jade counters.

I can feel the tears forming, "Jayson is all I know. I can't just give up because he made one mistake."

But it was more than that. I wasn't like Jade; yes her parents split up, but she always had two parents to come home to, and stability. If she and Max break up, she will still have her family. Besides Jayson, a mother thousands of miles away and a grandmother that's ill, I don't have anyone left. I can't just walk away from that.

Jade looks at me, "What makes you think it was only one mistake? And isn't one mistake enough?"

I shrug. *Is she right?*

Jade continues, "We love you girl, we're best friends. But you always have an opinion about what everyone else is doing. I can guarantee you that if this were Kara, you'd have a hell of a lot to say. Have you ever taken a look at your own situation?"

I sigh. This conversation was making my head spin. Kara can see that it was taking a toll on me and is instantly by my side.

"We're really worried about you Blair. But if this is what you want to do, I'll rock out with you," she says.

Jade joins us, sitting on the other side of me.

"Me too," she says giving me a soft nudge.

I quickly wipe the tears from my eyes, "Thanks guys."

By the time dinner is over we are stuffed. In an attempt to lighten the mood, Jade goes into the kitchen and prepares the cake she picked up while I send a quick text and Kara goes to the bathroom. Once she returns, Jade and I serenade her with our best rendition of "Happy birthday." Kara beams and closes her eyes to blow out the candles and make a wish.

Kara takes a bite of her double chocolate cake, "I'm so happy we got to do this! Thanks for celebrating my birthday with me ladies!"

"Of course boo. We have to make up for our last girl's night, staying indoors was way better," Jade giggles.

We all laugh at the memory of our last night out on the town with just us three. That night pretty much ended with Jade getting into a fight with her ex and his secret boyfriend, causing us to be carried out of gay nightclub.

We toast, "Here's to growth!"

While Kara and Jade continue talking and refill on champagne, I hear a knock at the door and quickly jump up to get it. My birthday surprise has finally arrived, and I lead him into the living room.

I announce, "The fun isn't over yet!"

The male stripper I paid for walks up to Kara and begins to dance.

Kara's eyes light up, "Oh my god!"

"You're the one that said you loved Magic Mike!" I tease.

Jade and I can't help but laugh and egg him on. We go for our purses and retrieve the dollar bills we brought along for the night. To Kara's surprise, the dark chocolate and oily man of steel peels off his clothes before picking her up and carefully laying her on the floor. The music picks up as Jade puts on "Pony" by Ginuwine, the ultimate male stripper song, thanks to the super sexy Channing Tatum. Man of steel then proceeds to gyrate in his G-string, effortlessly swinging his ten-inch penis in Kara's face. She looks horrified, and we can't hide our amusement. We laugh as we continue to throw ones.

She covers her face in embarrassment, "I hate you guys!"

6

I stare down at my ring and sigh; lately, it's starting to feel like the weight of the world is on my hand. Ever since Kara's birthday, I haven't talked to my friends much. It's not that I'm mad at them, but after my so-called intervention, I needed some time and space to process all that they had said. They were brutally honest with me, and it shook me to my core.

I adjust the bracelet that Jade got me and exhale heavily once more. Maybe she was right, I could dish it out all the judgment in the world, but I wasn't that great at taking it. I guess in a way; I was so brash because I didn't want them to make the same mistakes I did or to get hurt. To be honest, I feel extremely embarrassed. I don't like feeling that my friends can look at me and see how weak I've been. It's something I've tried to camouflage for so long, but right now I feel exposed.

I place a lit joint in my mouth and slowly inhale. After a moment, my body mellows out, and I'm able to relax a bit. I lie back on my bed pillows and look up at the ceiling, before taking another hit. Jayson comes into the bedroom interrupting my thoughts. He gets comfortable beside me in bed and turns on Netflix.

He turns to me, "What type of movie do you want to watch?"

I shrug, "Something scary?"

"So that you can have nightmares again?" Jayson teases.

I laugh, "Shut up; I can't help what I dream about."

He chuckles as he sifts through the movie options. He settles on a low-budget Indie horror film and hits play. About ten minutes into the movie, his phone rings and he reaches over to pick it up. As soon as he gets out of the bed and takes his phone into the other room, I know it's her. *Her.* My skin grows hot. I grab the remote and pause the movie. I feel my body tense up before glancing over at the bedside clock and seeing that it's just past midnight. *This bitch has some fucking nerve!* After a moment, Jayson returns and rejoins me in bed. He can sense my attitude almost immediately.

Shaking his head, he says, "Not tonight Blair."

"What do you mean not tonight? Then when?" I ask.

This entire situation was beyond unfair. It's like he faults me for being upset when he is the one that cheated. I'm the one that was deceived and lied to. Now I'm expected to walk on eggshells when she calls? It was complete bullshit.

I continue, "Why does she think it's ok to call you so late? Can't she show some damn respect for our relationship?"

Jayson rubs his temples, "Look, she isn't feeling well and may need to go to the hospital."

"So now what? You just drop your life whenever she calls?" I challenge.

He turns to me, "I will if it concerns my child."

My eyes scorch. I want to slap him with all of my might. It wasn't fair. *What did I do to deserve this?*

I cry, "So where does that leave me?"

I feel like I'm coming apart at the seams.

Jayson sighs, "Babe, I know this is hard. But you can't expect me to ignore anything that has to do with my child. What kind of man would I be?"

I sneer, "Oh so now this is your child? What about the DNA?"

He nods, "Until I see results that say otherwise, I'm not going to do that to that baby."

"Your baby," I mumble.

Jayson exhales heavily, "Listen to me, I love you, Blair, I'm going to marry you. I know it's hard right now. But we will get through this; I need you to trust me."

I can't believe this is my life. I look at him and have no idea how I even got here. He constantly placates me with promises that I know he simply can't keep. I don't know what's wrong with me and why I feel the need to put myself through this. Part of me wonders, is this love? Is this as good as it gets? What did I do? Where did I go wrong? How can he make me feel whole, yet also so broken? I've never felt further from myself than I do now.

I shake my head, "How could you do this to me?"

Now he was becoming annoyed.

Jayson rolls his eyes, "Look I'm not getting into this shit again."

We fall silent for a moment. Both too angry and stubborn to make a move. He reaches over and tries to pull me in for a hug. He always does this, trying to distract me with sex. I was unwilling to fall for it this time. After slapping away his hands, I quickly jump out of bed and wipe the tears from my eyes.

I scream, "I hate you!"

Enraged, I rip my pillow out of bed and stomp down the stairs into the living room. I pull out the spare blanket from the closet and wrap it around my body. My chest heaves with fury as I desperately try to calm my nerves. I walk over to the couch and plop down, eager to fall asleep and forget all of my despair. My heart continues to pump rapidly through my chest, and it feels like it's going to explode. I take a few deep breaths and try to relax, but all I can think about is how much I hate them both and how sick I am of the excuses and flat out disregard for me and my feelings. I stare out into the dark, thinking of ways to hurt them the way they hurt me. Before long, I'm fast asleep, dreaming of a better life, a happy one. A few hours later I feel his soft fingertips stroke my hair and I slowly open my eyes.

"I'm sorry babe; I know how hard this entire

situation has been on you. I'll tell her to stop calling so late," he whispers.

Still half asleep, I can see the torment on his face. I can't help but feel bad for him; I can only imagine what he's going through.

I say, "I'm sorry too."

"For what?"

"For saying I hate you. I don't," I confess.

He smiles, "Oh yea, that. It's ok; I know you don't mean it."

He leans down, giving me a soft kiss and hug. His hands trail up my thigh and squeeze my behind as he kisses me once more. This time the kiss is deeper, more passionate and fiery. I open myself to him and eagerly take him in. He swoops me up and carries me back upstairs into our bedroom. After gently laying me down on the bed, he carefully peels off my panties and nightshirt revealing my naked body. Without saying a word, he spreads my legs and indulges in my honey pot. I gasp as he works wonders with his tongue. He holds my legs open as I moan and squirm with pleasure. My head spins as if I'm intoxicated. I try to get lost in the feeling, but I can't help but think about the baby that he's having with another woman. He continues to lick and kiss my womanhood as hot tears stream down my face.

I love this man so much that it hurts. I hate him for having this type of power over me. For as much as I wanted to slap, kick and hurt him, I want to pull him close and get lost in every inch of his being. The constant back and forth of my heart drives me crazy.

Suddenly my body reacts, and I climax, crying out in ecstasy. I reach down and grab his face, eager to feel his lips on mine. He climbs on top of me as I wrap my legs around his torso. He pulls down his basketball shorts and places his tongue into my mouth as he enters me, causing me to cry out once more. He sees the tears on my face and kisses them away. I close my eyes and arch my back, welcoming every inch of him inside of me. My nails dig into his back as he continues to stroke in and out.

Then he weaves his fingers through my hair and whispers, "I love you."

"I love you too," I pant.

We continue to make love until we fall asleep.

The next day, I'm at Gran's apartment helping her with her beloved puzzles. It's one of her favorite things to do in her downtime, and she swears it keeps her memory razor sharp. I've always enjoyed helping her with them, even as a child. There are more than a hundred puzzle pieces scattered over the dining room table as she patiently sifts through them. I sit in the chair across from her twirling my fingers.

"You're awfully quiet today," she observes.

I look up, and she's eyeing me with suspicion. I sigh, knowing there's no point in trying to hide it.

I put my head in my hands, "Sorry Gran, I have a lot on my mind."

She asks, "Is this about you going to India?"

I quickly shake my head no, "Oh I don't think I'm going."

"Blair Gisele Montgomery! Why on earth would you not?"

I sigh, "Because I'm in a relationship and what do I look like just leaving?"

She looks confused, "Who said that you had to choose?"

I stay silent, focusing my attention on the puzzle.

"This is a once in a lifetime opportunity, you have to take advantage of it," she states.

"But what about you? Who will be here to help you if I leave?" I ask.

She waves me off, "I lived a full, happy life, and I'm a grown ass woman. I'll manage." Gran continues, "Don't let your life pass you by trying to be what others think you should be. You've got to live your life for you."

I nod, pondering what she said.

"You owe it to yourself to go after your dreams. You have so much potential, and you're such a beautiful person. Please give this a little more thought," she pleads.

"Thank you, Gran. I promise I will think about it," I reply.

I get up from my seat and walk into the kitchen. Gran made her infamous pound cake, and suddenly I can't stop thinking about it. I cut a slice before grabbing two twelve-ounce bottles of Dr. Pepper out of the fridge. After handing Gran one, I take a seat and bite into my cake.

"Thank you." Gran continues to pry, "So what else is

going on?"

I chuckle; of course, she knew there was more to what was bothering me. I swallow my cake and take a quick sip of my soda.

"It's just this entire engagement; I feel so lost," I vent.

She nods, "Are you having second thoughts? It's ok if you are."

Gran abruptly stops talking and lets out a hoarse cough. In an instant, I'm on my feet and by her side.

"Are you ok? Do you need some water?" I worry.

She shakes her head, "No baby I'm fine. Don't even think about changing the subject."

I sigh and shrug.

Gran wipes her mouth and takes a quick sip of her Dr. Pepper, "Well it seems to me that your head and heart are not on the same page. Are you sure Jayson is the one for you?"

Her question takes me aback.

I return to my seat and quickly nod, "Yes of course. He's all I know."

"But?" Gran pries.

"I just want to feel like he has my back. And lately, I don't feel like he does. He's hurt me so much. I don't know if I can ever love him the same again," I confess.

"So why are you putting yourself through all of this?" she questions.

"I love him, and relationships have problems right? I mean did you and Pop have a perfect relationship?" I ask.

"Child no, we had our ups and downs like any

relationship. They all have problems from time to time, but one thing I know is that love doesn't hurt," Gran explains.

I stare down at my ring finger. *Love doesn't hurt.*

Later that evening, I wander the King of Prussia Mall eager to forget some of my woes with a few new purchases. I make my way into the Free People store and browse the jean section. It always felt good to treat myself, and it's been quite a while since I did. Although I appreciated fashion, I'm not one to get all done up every day like Jade and Kara. Most of the time, I was perfectly content wearing a pair of ripped jeans and a comfortable t-shirt. But every now and again, I loved to get dressed up and slay some labels. A nice pair of wide leg denim pants catches my eye, and I lift them off the rack.

"Would you like to try those on?" a soft voice asks.

I turn to see a friendly and familiar face, "Heather? Oh my goodness, how are you?"

"Blair? I swear you haven't aged one bit!" Heather beams.

We share a brief hug.

"It's so good to see you! What's it been? Like two years?" I ask.

She nods, "Yes something like that. Isn't it crazy how fast time flies?"

I chuckle, "Girl I can't keep up half the time. So what's new with you?"

"Nothing special, going to graduate school and working here on the side. You know every little bit helps," she explains.

"Grad school? That's major! Congratulations!" I exclaim.

"I'm just trying to make it out here," Heather says.

I nod, "Yes I get it, trust me."

She changes the subject, "So how are things going with your art? You're so talented, and I've always loved your work! When is the next show?"

Once she brings up my art show my heart sinks. I can't bear to tell her that my work has staggered and a show was nowhere on the horizon. To be honest, I feel embarrassed more than anything else. I always appreciated the love I received from others with regards to my work. Although I painted mainly as a means of personal expression, knowing that others could take a peek into my world and like what they saw meant a lot to me. The fact that I've let my gift grow idle felt like I was letting everyone else, including myself down.

"As soon as I finish getting all of my pieces done," I lie.

Heather seems pleased, "Well let me know because I'll definitely come and show some support!"

I smile, "Will do."

She leads me towards the dressing room, and I proceed to try on my jeans. After finding the perfect size along with other accessories, I make my way to the register to check out.

"It was so nice seeing you! We have to stay in

touch," Heather says as she rings up my items.

I smile and take out my iPhone, "We definitely should, what's your number?"

She swiftly gives me her contact information, and I store it on my cell. We hug once more before I leave, ready to go home and relax for the rest of the day. But as I get into my car and secure my seatbelt, my phone rings.

"Hello?"

"You still mad at us trick?" Jade says.

I chuckle, "No, what do you want?"

"Kara and I are about to go to the movies and wanted to see if you'd like to come," she explains.

The movies sounded like a great idea. I can't remember the last time I've been.

"Sure, what are you going to see?" I ask.

"That new movie with Idris Elba, girl Kara is determined to see her man on the screen," Jade laughs.

I can't help but snicker to myself. Kara made it no secret how much she lusted for the British actor. Jade gives me the information to the movie theater, and I head in that direction. Even though it's only been a week, I missed my friends. Seeing them would definitely lift my spirits.

I hurry into the Ritz movie theater, and to my pleasant surprise, I see my friends waiting patiently in the lobby. *They're on time for once!* I always loved this theater, it was small, intimate, and had a vintage charm to it. Once my friends see me, they both give me warm hugs before dragging me into the theater. Kara, being her usual crazy self, smuggled some liquor and snacks into the theater with her large Louis Vuitton purse. Giving us the chance to watch the movie while enjoying an array of sweets coupled with a strong cranberry and vodka cocktails.

By the end of the movie, we are all tipsy and in no rush to go home. Instead, we decide to take a walk and enjoy the beauty of Society Hill. A popular part of Philadelphia, decorated with cobblestone streets and historic homes that was often visited by tourists. We make our way past Washington Square before coming up on a quaint bridal boutique nestled in between family dentistry and law office. I stare at the elegant wedding dresses in the display window. The designs are vast and beautiful. I can't help but wonder what type of bride I would be. I stand there, admiring the timeless dresses and hopeful about my own wedding day.

"You want to go inside?" Jade asks, interrupting my thoughts.

I can see that she's trying to be supportive and it really means a lot. I contemplate her question for a moment. This is something I've looked forward to for as long as I can remember. I always dreamed of doing this with not only my best friends but also with my Gran and mother by my side. My friends watch me, waiting for my answer. I slowly nod my head yes. I figure this could be a test run. I am engaged; after all, I'd have to look for a dress at some point. We enter the shop and are immediately greeted by a warm employee.

"Hi ladies, welcome to Bella Bridal. What can I help you with today?" she says.

Jade replies, "Our friend is getting married and wants

to try on some dresses."

Her face lights up, "Who's the lucky girl?"

I feel myself become nervous.

Kara gives me a nudge, "Blair here, she just got engaged."

"Well, congratulations! I'm sure this is a very exciting period of your life. My name is Eva; I'll be more than happy to assist you in any way that I can. Do you have an idea of the type of look you're going for?"

I shrug, "No not really. I'm only looking right now."

She smiles, "I understand, finding the perfect dress can be a process! Don't worry; we just got a new shipment of our spring line in, I have quite a few pieces I think that you'd enjoy."

For some reason, I not as excited as I thought I should be. If anything I feel overwhelmed, this was not how I imagined this feeling like at all. *Is this normal?* Nonetheless, I plant a smile on my face and follow Eva towards the back of the boutique with my friends. She tells us to take a seat and offers us all a glass of champagne. Of course, we accept. I watch as she brings the latest bridal designs out on full display. There were so many options that it makes my head spin. When she finally pulls out an elegant backless mermaid gown, my friends and I gasp. It's perfect; the beaded detailing added a modern touch to such a classic look.

Eva encourages, "I think that this will look phenomenal on you."

Kara and Jade quickly agree, ordering me to try it on at once. My heart pumps through my chest, and I swear it becomes harder to breathe. I take a final sip of my champagne and rise out of my seat to follow Eva into the changing room. She delicately hangs the dress up on the wall rack.

She smiles, "If you need assistance, please give me a shout."

"Thank you," I say.

Once she leaves, I remove my clothing before unhooking the dress from its satin hanger. I hear a soft knock on the door and quickly open it.

Jade peeks inside, "Do you need help?"

I nod. She steps inside, helping me step into my dress.

"I want to see!" Kara calls out.

After a moment, she enters the dressing room with us as Jade zips me up.

Kara admires, "Oh Blair, you look amazing."

We step back out into the showroom and Eva's eyes light up. She helps me up onto the pedestal situated in the middle of the room and turns me towards the floor length vanity mirror. I'm shocked at the woman staring back at me. I can see my friends behind me, in complete awe. Suddenly my stomach aches and my head spins. I feel woozy like I'm on a bad roller coaster ride. My eyes dart towards the floor, I can't look any longer.

Eva comes up behind me, "This looks like a perfect fit. You will barely need any adjustments!"

She places her hands on my shoulders, and I flinch.

"Oh my goodness! You're burning up honey," she observes.

"Please help me take this off!" I order.

My friends are at my side in an instant.

"What's wrong?" Jade worries.

"Blair, you're sweating like crazy," Kara says.

The more they talked, the more nauseous I become. I quickly step down off the pedestal and lose my balance. Luckily, Jade and Eva catch me before I fall. Without saying another word, they swiftly help me into the dressing room and out of the dress. I stand there only in my underwear for a moment, trying to catch my breath.

7

Jayson and I are fighting again. It's been three days, and things aren't getting any better between us. Neither one of us is willing to back down. This morning I mentioned India, and it was World War III. Angelique reached out the night before to follow up like most professionals do and I couldn't bring myself to answer and turn down the opportunity. Instead, I brought it to Jayson's attention hoping to reach some sort of compromise. But to my dismay, all he did was give me an ultimatum. Things escalated pretty quickly from there; he yelled, and I screamed. Naturally infuriated, I stormed out of the house and drove to Jade's, who is conveniently out of town at the moment. In an attempt to make up for ruining their trip to Costa Rica last summer, she decided to take Max to Mexico for his birthday. When she asked me to feed Blu while she was away for the week, I was more than happy to oblige.

"Hey Blu," I say as I enter the apartment.

He's at my feet in an instant, rubbing his body along my ankles. I can tell that he misses his mom and craved some company. I lock the door behind me and head straight for the kitchen. After pulling his food out of the cupboard and setting everything up, I get comfortable on the living room couch. Rather than be in a rush to return home, I reach for the remote and turn on the television, eager to find something interesting to watch. After mindlessly flipping through the channels, I finally settle on an Oprah Winfrey documentary and get comfortable.

A few hours later, I still have no desire to leave. I pull myself up off the seat and decide to light a few candles and turn on some music. After retrieving one of my trusty joints and sparking it up, I turn off the television, lie back onto the couch and close my eyes. The music takes over and consumes my thoughts. When "Emotional Rollercoaster" by Vivian Green plays, each lyric resonates deeply with my life. I painfully sing along with tears streaming down my face, only stopping to take another hit of my weed.

I don't know when I became this weak, but I hated it more than anything. I've yearned for and craved stability for so long. Being with Jayson gave me the security I always thought I needed. I'm not like my friends, being alone scares the shit out of me. Having a family of my own is something I dreamt about ever since I was a little girl. Deep down, I know that Jayson doesn't deserve me.

No, I wasn't perfect and yes I was flawed, but I've been a damn good woman to him. Even forsaking myself and the ones closest to me in the process. And what do I have to show for it? The promise of a better life that he attached to this ring? To be honest, I don't know if the promise is enough anymore. *But who was I if I wasn't his?* I sit up, feeling extremely annoyed with myself. *I sound so pathetic!*

Back at home, Jayson is gone, and I'm slightly relieved. I still had a lot on my mind and wasn't in the mood for another disagreement. I walk into my studio and look through my paintings, admiring the work I've done. After taking a seat in front of my blank canvas, I just stare at it. The words of my Gran and friends play over and over again in my mind. For some reason, all of my fears are coming to the surface. For so long, I clung to the idea of being someone's girlfriend. But I'm more than that. I'm an artist, it's always been my calling, it's my passion, and I fell in love with it far before I ever knew of Jayson. Deep down I know that I'm not done with it, I still have more that I wanted to share with the world. I'm tired of waiting; this changes today. I pick up a jar of black paint along with my favorite paintbrush and let my hand move freely. An hour or so later, my fingers are covered in paint, and I couldn't be happier. It's not perfect, but it's a start. I gaze at my painting before wiping off my hands and reaching for my phone. For the first time in a long time, I know exactly what I want and I what I'm going to do. Before I can stop myself, I type up an email and quickly hit send.

Later that week, I walk into the salon, anxious to get my hair done. Jayson and I finally made up and decided to have a night out on the town to lay our issues to rest. It's Valentine's Day after all; a day when most couples can put aside their differences and come together to celebrate the love they share. I wanted no different for Jayson and me, and I'd much rather spend the night enjoying one another other than fighting. Although I hated when we didn't see eye to eye, I loved when we made up. Tonight was going to be a great one.

The receptionist smiles and asks me to take a seat as she takes my coat. I pick up the latest copy of *Essence* magazine and mindlessly flip through the pages while I wait. A couple of minutes later, my stylist Tania, greets me and promptly walks me to the back of the salon. I take a seat in the wash chair as she drapes a soft white towel over my shoulders. After instructing me to lean my head back, I close my eyes and do as I'm told. In no time, she goes to work. Her hands massage my scalp and relax my nerves while washing away all the dirt and oil.

"So how have you been boo?" Tania asks.

Since coming to her a few months ago, Tania has been a breath of fresh air. She's very friendly, and we always have great conversations while she does my hair. Even though she's about five years younger, she's always extremely professional and accommodating to her clients. I don't trust many people with my hair, but with her, I don't have a worry in the world. Her mantra is healthy hair first, and she treats my hair like she would her own. In a society full of hairstylists that are more than eager to take your money, she was a rare find.

"I'm good. Just ready for spring," I say.

She agrees, "Girl who are you telling? I swear if it snows one more time. I'm over it being so cold. I'm ready to bring out my sandals and hoochie outfits."

We both share a laugh as she combs through my curls, making sure to distribute the conditioner throughout my tresses evenly.

"So do you have any Valentine's Day plans?" she asks.

I nod, "Dinner tonight."

"Nice! Where at?"

"I'm not sure; he told me it's a surprise," I explain.

"That's so romantic. You have a good man girl; these clowns out here know nothing about romance. Consider yourself lucky," Tania says.

I slightly smile. *I guess she's right.*

As she rinses my hair, some water splashes onto my eye, I quickly reach up to wipe the excess water away with my towel.

She gasps, "Is that what I think it is?"

"Huh?" I ask, truly puzzled.

"Blair! Is that an engagement ring?"

I sit up and allow her to pat my hair dry with the towel. I look at my finger and take notice of the rock I seemed to have completely forgotten about. I'm pretty surprised that she didn't notice the ring when I first got engaged.

I nod, "Yes."

"Oh my god! Congratulations! I bet you're so excited!" Tania beams.

She pulls me up and gives me a warm hug. Her excitement surprises me. Not many shared her same enthusiasm, myself included. Nonetheless, it feels good to know that someone is sincerely happy for me and my relationship. We walk to her chair, and I take a seat. Tania proceeds to carefully parting my hair into sections and blow-drying.

"Your hair is getting so long Blair! Nice and healthy too. You better not cut it! I won't allow it," she lectures.

I giggle, "No way, only trims."

Suddenly, a rush of cold air comes into the shop as the door swings open. A woman treks over to the receptionist to check in. As she removes her hat and coat, I freeze. *It's her.*

Of all the salons in Philadelphia, Renee just had to walk into this one. *Why? Why? Why?* She hands her belongings to the receptionist, and I quickly look at the floor, refusing to give her any of my attention. I stay silent as Tania trims my ends. I can hear her being greeted by her stylist and they walk towards the back to the washing area. As she approaches, I try my best to avoid eye contact, but I can't help but look at her when she passes. It only takes her a millisecond to realize who I am. Her eyes stare daggers at me, and the tension is thick.

"So have you two set a date yet?" Tania asks.

I can tell by the look in Renee's eyes that she knows

what Tania is talking about. But before she can react, her stylist leads her away.

I exhale slightly and say, "No not yet,"

"Well, when you decide, let me know! I will definitely hook your hair up," Tania says.

I loved her, but at this moment I did not want to talk about this. The palms of my hands grow sweaty, and I can feel my ears are blazing. I feel like I'm going to be sick.

"Do you mind if I go to the bathroom?" I ask.

"Sure thing boo," she nods.

Tania removes my cape and points me towards the back of the salon to the restroom. Once inside, I quickly lock the door behind me. *I will not react.* I try to coach myself. A large part of me wants to confront her. I want to know why it was my man that she decided to have a baby with. After some contemplation, I refuse to do that. Because as much as I dislike her, she owes me nothing. This is all Jayson's fault. His lies and deceitful ways created this mess. I'm going to be his wife soon, and that means accepting all of him, even this baby if it's his. No matter how much I hate it, Renee comes with the package. I wash my hands and splash some water on my face. After taking a few deep breaths and drying my face and hands, I put my best calm mask on. Once I open the door, I'm startled by Renee standing only a few inches from me.

"Can I talk to you for a second?" she asks.

I slowly nod. She crosses her arms; her belly is poking out through her blush sweater. She looks tired;

I'm sure being pregnant can take a lot out of a person. Part of me feels bad for her (a very small part); this situation wasn't ideal for anyone.

I try my best to be civilized, "What's up?"

"I know you don't like me, but this baby is going to be here whether you like it or not," Renee says.

My heart wrenches. My nightmare is becoming more and more of a reality. Hearing her actually say those words stung. The fact that I had no control or say so about such a damaging situation in my life pissed me off.

"I understand that," I murmur.

She continues, "I'm sorry about the way things happened. But you can't get in the way of Jayson being a father to this child. Forcing him to marry you doesn't change that."

Her voice makes my skin crawl. I swear if she weren't pregnant, I probably would've snatched her up by her neck and squeezed with all of my might. I take a deep breath once more to calm my nerves.

"I'm not trying to," I reply.

"Then why are you making things so difficult? Let him leave, he doesn't want to be with you anymore," she snorts.

I almost choke on my own saliva, "What?"

"He tells me everything. How you stalk him and threaten to kill yourself if he leaves."

What the fuck? I can't believe my ears. Only Jayson and Gran knew about my cutting. Yes, it was a dark time in my life but I never once tried taking my life, especially to try and keep a man. I can feel Renee watching me.

"What? Do you not see this ring on my finger? You think I proposed to myself?" I charge.

"I mean what do you expect when you give a man that type of ultimatum?" Renee argues.

"You sound crazy," I say shaking my head.

She doesn't back down, "Oh do I?"

"Yes! Jayson is a grown ass man. Yea, you guys, had something, and as a result, a baby is on the way. I've accepted that. But clearly he wants to be with me, a one night stand and a baby isn't going to come between what we have," I rebut.

Just then, Tania appears.

"Everything alright?" she asks.

I nod, "Yes, sorry."

I quickly follow her and go back to my chair where she begins straightening my hair. As soon as she was finished, I go to the receptionist to pay, making sure to leave Tania a generous tip. By now, Renee is in her stylist's chair, and we don't even look in each other's direction. To be honest, I prefer it that way. As much as I refuse to let her get a rise out of me, the thought of pounding her face seems way too tempting. Instead, I bundle up and make my way out the door into the brisk winter cold. Once I reach my car, I hop inside and call Jayson right away. Luckily for him, he doesn't answer.

My phone rings, pulling me out of my nap. Somehow I fell asleep waiting for Jayson to get home. Since bumping into Renee at the salon, I haven't heard from him. In a few hours that will all change and I definitely plan on giving him a piece of my mind before dinner. The more I think about our encounter, the queasier I get. Her words repeating over and over again like a bad song in my mind. I reach across my bed to grab my phone, and an unfamiliar number pops across my screen.

"Hello?" the sleep still clings to my voice.

"Hi, is this Blair Montgomery?"

I sit up, "Yes this is her."

"This is Julie with Jefferson Hospital; we had a Loretta Montgomery checked in about an hour ago. She listed you as her emergency contact," she explains.

My heart races, "What's going on?"

Julie provides me with more details and I quickly jot down Gran's room information before hanging up. I dash into the bathroom to splash some water on my face, grab the first clothes I see and head straight there.

At the hospital, I enter the room and see my grandmother with what seems like a million different tubes in and out of her. She looks tired, different. I instantly approach her.

"What happened?" I ask the attending nurse.

She can see the worry on my face, "She lost consciousness, and we suspect that it's due to a cardiac obstruction."

I panic, "What does that mean? She'll get better right?"

"We will try our best. Right now she just needs to take it easy and rest up."

Gran sleeps as I nervously cross my arms and try to remain rational. Once the nurse leaves, I pull out my cell and call my mother. She doesn't answer, so I leave her a message. Next, I call Jayson, but his phone goes to voicemail again. I leave him a message in addition to a text asking to call me back as soon as possible. I get in the seat next to my grandmother's bed and stay by her side. Moments later, she shifts in her bed and slowly opens her eyes.

"Hey baby," she whispers, her voice still a little raspy.

I smile and grab her hand, "Hey you."

"Stay strong," she coughs.

Then she goes back to sleep. An hour passes before Jayson finally calls me back. Not wanting to disturb Gran, I answer my phone and step into the waiting room lobby.

"What's up babe?" he says.

"Why haven't you been answering my calls?"

Jayson replies, "Because I'm at work, it's been a crazy ass day."

"Look, we need to talk. I ran into Renee, and she had a lot to say about you," I accuse.

"Blair look I'm not in the mood for these games right now. We are supposed to be going to dinner tonight, let's not spoil it over something that doesn't even matter," he says.

I challenge him, "Oh, now it doesn't matter?"

I can hear him suck his teeth through the phone. To be honest, I wasn't in the mood to argue with him, so I opt to change the subject.

"We may have to take a rain check on dinner. Gran

fainted earlier and is in the hospital," I explain.

"Shit! Is she ok?" he worries.

I shrug, "I think so. I have to be here with her."

"I understand babe. I'll be there as soon as I get off," Jayson says.

My eyes water, "Ok."

"I love you," he states.

"I love you too," I reply.

I give him the room information before we hang up. My mouth feels extremely dry, like it's full of cotton, making it hard to swallow. I walk up to the vending machine and purchase a bottle of water. After taking a long sip, I turn on my feet and head back towards Gran's room. Suddenly, I see a wave of nurses and doctors rushing in that same direction.

I feel myself freeze as I watch them try to save her. I hear one of the nurses say cardiac arrest and I lose it. I scream out to my Gran and try to push my way through the hospital employees to be by her side. It takes three nurses to hold me back. After a few minutes and unanswered cries, one of the doctors approaches me with a somber look on his face.

He places a sympathetic hand on my shoulder, "I'm sorry, we lost her."

My world turns black. It feels as though my heart has been ripped out of my chest. I drop my phone, and the screen shatters onto the hard cold tile. *She's dead. She's dead.* I pinch myself praying that it's a dream. But I wince at the pain. My heart, my Gran, my everything is gone. The realization is too much to bear. I let out an unrecognizable scream and drop down to my knees. My world, my life is forever changed.

8

My week passes in a blur. When I'm not crying, I'm forced to plan a funeral. It's like the world is moving around me, but I'm stuck in place; trying to put the shattered pieces of my life back together. At Gran's apartment, I pack away her things and sort through old family photos. We had so many great memories together. I stare at my favorite photograph, a picture taken when I was about eight. My legs were stick thin, my hair was in two braided pigtails, and my smile was big. I was seated on my father's lap, and my mom has her arms around his neck smiling for the camera at my grandparent's old house. Gran had her arm wrapped around Pop, and we were all together and happy. The memory makes me smile. Although I hate that she's gone, I find comfort in knowing that she's been reunited with her dear husband and son. I relive those last few moments with Gran daily; regretting that I didn't cherish my time with her.

Days creep by, and I can barely keep myself together. Before I know it, I'm watching them bury my beloved grandmother. My mother, who returned to Philly as soon as the news broke, stays by my side, offering me all the comfort and assistance I need. She was forever grateful to my Gran for being there to take care of me when she couldn't, and she always had the utmost respect for her. She reassuringly places her hand on my shoulder as the overseeing pastor says one final prayer. When they begin to lower the casket, my heart races. Jayson can see my sorrow and gently weaves his fingers into mine. Tears cascade down my face as I try to keep my composure.

At the wake, I'm numb. The country club is beautiful, and the staff is more than accommodating, but all I want to do is lock myself in a room and cry myself to sleep. Clearly, I'm no stranger to losing someone, but it's never easy. When my father died, I didn't know how I would get through it. My Gran helped me so much, and it hurt to know that she was no longer here to be my strength and voice of reason. The thought makes my head spin, and I don't want to be around anyone.

I retreat into the bathroom and lock myself inside. For some reason, the bathroom was one of my favorite places to hide from my problems. I stare at myself in the large vanity mirror. My wrist tingles with anxiety, and I know my body is craving that familiar feeling of relief. As soon as the thought crosses my mind, I swear I can hear

Gran in my head telling me to be strong. I sigh and quickly dismiss that idea from my mind. She was right. I could be, and I would be strong, especially for her.

I splash some water into my face before returning to the main dining room. Jade sits beside me and places a cup of tea down in front of me while Kara fixes me a plate of food. My friends have been super attentive, helping with any and everything I need. Without them, my mother, and Jayson I'm not sure this funeral would've come together the way it did. I'm thankful to them for being my support system during this dark time in my life. I can't wait for this day to be over.

After being hugged and greeted by an abundance of sympathetic distant relatives and family friends, it feels like my chest is beginning to cave in. I need air; I feel like I'm suffocating. I rush outside onto the patio and take a deep breath, the cold winter air stinging my lungs.

"You alright?" Kai asks.

He startles me, but I stay silent. I give him a solemn look before turning back and looking out into the surrounding snow-covered trees.

"Do you want to be left alone?"

I slowly shake my head no. Kai instantly closes the patio door behind him and joins me outside. We stay quiet for a bit, staring out onto the landscape. I'm grateful that he gave me a moment of peace and quiet; it's soothing. An abrupt strong wind takes us both by surprise as if it's a frigid slap in the face. We turn and look at each other once more.

"I'm really sorry about your Gran. Kara told me how

close you two were." He continues, "I know it's hard right now, but you'll get through this. You're stronger than you know."

I stare at him and can see the sincerity in his eyes. For some odd reason, I feel myself get nervous.

I sniffle, "It doesn't feel like it."

He softly grins, "You are, trust me."

I smile, "Thanks, Kai."

To my surprise, he pulls me in for a hug, and I hug him back. He felt good, safe. I hadn't felt that in a long time. I realize it's because I trust him, I believe every word he said. I forgot what that felt like. When we pull away, I see Jayson through the glass glaring at us.

On the way home, the tension in the car is thick. I stay silent and look out the passenger window, watching the snowflakes as they begin to coat the city streets.

Jayson fumes, "So what was that about?"

"What?" I murmur.

He continues, "Why is that dude Kai always in your face? You used to fuck with him or something?"

I can't believe my ears. *This man has some fucking nerve!*

I argue, "Jayson, are you seriously asking me that right now? Today of all days?"

He hesitates, "I don't like the way he looks at you."

I shake my head. It feels like he's accusing me of something. Like I'd ever stoop as low as he did.

I yell, "My goodness, you are so fucking selfish! I just watched them bury my grandmother, and you're really coming at me with this bullshit? He's my best friend's little brother. What the hell is wrong with you?"

I can tell that he feels bad. When he tries to place an apologetic hand on my thigh, I smack it away.

I try my best to hold back my tears, "Please take me home."

Three days later, my mother is scheduled to head back to Brazil and insists on treating me to lunch before her flight. At Parc, I pick over my steak frites as my mother does her best to try and cheer me up. She's her usual self, vibrant and never feeling down for too long. The wait staff, like most people, are captured by her unique style and beauty. A few shades or so lighter than me, her auburn colored hair is big and wild. Many people think she looks like Erykah Badu, especially today. Their styles are very similar, to say the least. She's wearing a ninja-like topknot with the rest of her hair out while donning large hoop earrings and an oversized grey sweatshirt. Her bright orange bellbottoms commanded the attention in the room as soon as we entered the restaurant. During my visits with her, she always encouraged me to express myself and be comfortable with who I was no matter what others thought. My friends thought I was eccentric, but I had nothing on my mom. I remember the first time they met her, much like everyone else, they were mesmerized.

"I'm worried about you Blair," my mother confesses.

I take a sip of my cocktail and nibble on a piece of buttered bread.

"I'll be alright mom, don't worry. I miss Gran and Dad so much. I feel like I don't have anyone left," I explain.

"I know this is hard right now, but believe me you're not alone. I'm your mother; I'll always be here for you. I'm so sorry if you ever felt like I wasn't, but I am. Just say the word," she assures me.

When I look into her eyes, I can see that they are laced with guilt. In the past, I struggled with my anger towards her, especially as a rebellious hypersensitive teenager. Back then, I didn't know how to deal with all that pent-up emotion in a healthy way, not until I found my love of art. As an adult, I've come to appreciate and understand exactly who my mother is. And although I don't always agree with all of her choices, I don't love her any less. I needed her to know that I didn't blame or resent her. After all, we are all we had now.

I reach out and touch her hand, "I know."

She holds on tight and places my hand on her cheek. I can see tears forming in her eyes.

"So when should we start shopping for wedding dresses?" she says, changing the subject.

I softly pull my hand back and pick up another French fry. Memories of my recent panic attack flood my thoughts.

I shrug, "We haven't even set a date yet."

"No pressure! When you do, just let me know, and I'll be here. I'm so excited that you two are finally tying the knot! Eight years is long enough," she jokes.

I force a grin before taking another sip of my

cocktail. Jayson was the last person I wanted to discuss, especially with her leaving soon.

"How are things with you?" I ask.

She smiles, "Things are good. Richard just bought a damn yacht and wants to sail along Rio."

I chuckle, "That sounds like its right up your alley."

"You know me so well," she smiles. "Maybe you can come visit this summer, and we take it for a spin."

The idea sounds tempting.

"I'd love that," I say.

We order another round of drinks and continue to catch up. It felt good to spend this time together and enjoy each other's company. After lunch, I offer to take my mom to the airport, but she insists that I go home to get rest. After we share a long hug and kiss, I hail my mom a cab and kiss her once more.

"I love you, mom. Thanks for being here," I say.

My mother smiles, "I love you too, I'll call you when I land."

I help her into the cab before returning to my car and going home.

I wake from my nap tormented. I didn't realize how drunk I was until I got home and passed out in my bedroom. I have officially hit rock bottom. I feel as though I have nothing. I feel like nothing. I feel nothing.

Seeing my mom was amazing and it felt good to know that I had her in my corner. That reassurance wasn't enough to make up for the dread I feel now because she's gone too. The loneliness haunts me, and I can't think or see straight. I pull out the picture of my family and me from under my pillow and cry uncontrollably. I miss them all so much I would give anything just to hear their voices once more. About fifteen minutes later, my eyes are swollen from crying. I reluctantly pull myself out of bed and walk through the house. I notice Jayson isn't around; something that has become the norm once again. Part of me doesn't even care anymore. My stomach growls and I regret not eating all of my lunch. I walk into the kitchen and open the fridge but quickly close it. I have no desire to cook and want to eat something that I know would make me feel better. I pick my phone up off the counter and call Jayson. It rings with no answer, so I shoot him a quick text.

Blair: HEY WHERE ARE YOU? DO YOU MIND STOPPING BY THE STORE TO GET SOME COOKIES AND STRAWBERRY ICE CREAM?

I hit send and mindlessly wander my home. As a force of habit, I start tidying up the place. Since Gran passed, I paid little attention to basic things like keeping my house in order. As I was putting the last of the dishes in the dishwasher, my phone rings. It's a text. I quickly pick it up to see Jayson's reply. Once my eyes fixate on the image my heart stops, and I feel like I can't breathe.

This text isn't from Jayson at all. It was definitely from his phone, but he never in his right mind would send me this. I play the video, and it's Renee, naked, lying next to Jayson. She wickedly smiles at the camera as she films Jayson, who is fast asleep. From what it looks like, he is barely clothed himself. Just as I try to pick my jaw up off the floor, another text comes through.

Jayson: DO I LOOK LIKE A 1-NIGHT STAND?

I read the words over and over again. Each time my skin boiling over with rage. Ever since bumping into Renee, something didn't sit right with me. I hadn't had much time to revisit our encounter or what she said to me. But now everything is playing over in my mind as clear as day. Before I can respond, more texts flood my phone. Screenshots of their texts messages detailing the ins and outs of their relationship.

My heart stops when I see that what she told me was true. Text after text, I see my fiancé beg and plead with another woman to stay in his life. I can't even reply. How could I? What more is there to say? Suddenly, it dawns on me that he wanted us both and she seemed to be perfectly fine with that. Sister wives, just like Jade said. The realization that he looked me in my face time and time again and lied to me day in and day out makes me tremble. When I thought he was at doctor's appointments with her, he was laid up with her. This wasn't a one-night stand; it was an affair that carried on for damn near a year. All those nights I stayed up worrying and wondering where he was, he was with her. The truth makes my stomach turn. My friends were right; he's no good. He took my love and all that I am for granted, turning his back on me and crawling to another woman when I needed him the most. This man played me for a fool for the last motherfucking time.

I snatch my engagement ring off and slam it onto the counter top. After storming upstairs, I go straight to his closet. Pulling and ripping out all of his belongings and throwing them onto the floor. It wouldn't be long before he was back and I would have a surprise for him waiting. He had no idea.

A few hours later, my home looks like a war zone. I tore through all of Jayson's belongings, ripping his clothes to shreds. Any framed picture that I came across was bashed into the floor and destroyed. I felt nothing but rage. I was so infuriated that I couldn't even bring myself to shed a tear. My tears had officially run out, and I was done. I no longer cared about him or his feelings. I wanted to feel good. And fucking his shit up felt strangely liberating. By the time Jayson comes home, I feel much calmer, stoic even. As he walks through the door, I'm quietly sitting in the dark living room drinking a glass of red wine.

He calls out to me, "Blair! Blair where are you?"

The upheaval probably has him worried. It looks like our house was ransacked by a bunch of home invaders. I ignore his calls and light up a joint, startling him. When he sees me he calms for a moment, but then his look becomes confused.

"What happened?" he asks, making his way over to me.

I smirk, "Oh you don't know?"

Jayson quickly shakes his head. He's acting delirious, and it's really getting under my skin.

"Is everything alright?"

I ignore his question, "Where have you been?"

I know that I'm about to hear another lie. But I need him to lie to my face one more time. It's different when you actually know someone is lying. I want him to confirm what I already knew deep down in my heart for so long.

"Oh I was at the gym playing ball with the guys," he swiftly answers.

There it is.

"Oh really?" I ask.

Jayson takes a seat beside me, "Yea. What's up? Why do you look like that?"

I take a hit of my weed and close my eyes. Then I reach for my glass of Merlot and take a long sip. I can tell that my behavior is making him weary, torturing him with the suspense almost. It feels empowering to be in control for once.

Finally, I ask, "I guess you never got my text earlier?"

His eyes slightly twitch, but he maintains his cool, "My phone died, it must not have gone through. What did I miss?"

I say, "Why don't you ask Renee?"

Almost instantly, his eyes grow big.

He stutters, "What? What are you talking about?"

Like I expected, another damn lie. I quickly put out my joint and turn to him.

"You know exactly what the fuck I'm talking about! I know you were just with her you lying son of a bitch!" I yell.

He looks surprised, but he maintains his story, "Babe, I know you've been going through a lot right now, but you're really tripping."

That was enough to set me over the edge.

I quickly pick up my phone and pull up Renee's video and shove it into his face, "Then explain this!"

He sits there dumbfounded, unsure of what to do or say next.

I continue, "You really are a piece of shit. Do you know that? You allowed me to drive myself crazy for years, making me feel like an asshole for having suspicions when I was right the entire time. So how many other bitches were your fucking Jayson? Cause I know, she's not the only one."

He stays silent and sinks his head into his hands.

"You are such a coward. I want you out. Get your shit and get the fuck out of my life!" I scream.

I take the ring off the table and throw it in his face. He catches it, and his eyes turn red.

"Blair," he begs.

He looks at me pleading for a moment. But I am through with it all; nothing more can be said, nothing more can be done.

"I took the liberty of packing your stuff, well whatever I didn't destroy. Your bags are by the door. You have two minutes to get your shit and get out of here, or things will get really fucking ugly," I order.

I rise from the couch, go up to our bedroom and lock the door behind me. I can hear him cursing at my destruction, and I could care less. Luckily for Jayson, he obeys my wishes and leaves once and for all. I was free, and it felt good.

9

The last weeks of winter continue to linger. However the snow finally began melting away, signifying another season coming to an end, soon to be forgotten with the rest of them. I emerge from the house for the first time in days and take a deep breath. I can feel spring on the tip of my nose. It was only a matter of time before the flowers would start to bloom and the days become longer. I hop into my car and pull off in a hurry to meet my friends.

The realization that the last few years of my life were a lie ate through me. Thoughts of all that I gave and was willing to give for the sake of not being alone made me sick to my stomach. Jayson played me because I allowed him to. It's that simple. Somewhere down the line, the fearless girl I once was evaporated and morphed into a scared woman clinging to her own twisted idea of love. I don't think I've ever been more disappointed in myself. Gran was right; love doesn't hurt. More specifically, love damn sure doesn't lie or cheat.

At Honey's, I request a table for three and am promptly seated by a friendly hostess. It's no surprise that I'm the first one there. My friends are always late, especially Jade. Being the first one to arrive was something I've grown accustomed to over the years. I take a seat and pull out my phone to check my notifications. I'm pleasantly surprised to see an email from Angelique Graves. My heart races as I open the thread.

> **To: Blair Montgomery**
> **From: Angelique Graves**
> **Subject: Re: Teaching Opportunity**
>
> **Hello Blair!**
>
> **I'm so happy to see that you reached out to me. Please accept my apology for the delayed response. I've been traveling pretty extensively lately and haven't had a chance to sort through my emails.**
> **That being said, I'm absolutely thrilled to hear that you will be joining us in India this spring! I know that you will be a great addition to our team and the children will stand to learn a great deal from you.**

We plan on leaving March 25th and returning June 15th. I have attached all the necessary disclosures and documents. Please take a moment to review, sign, and send back to me within the week. Once you do, we will get your flight and other accommodations booked. I'd recommend making an appointment with your doctor to get all the required vaccinations as soon as possible! Let me know if you have any questions.

See you in a few weeks!
Angie

I re-read the message and can't mask my excitement. I'm so glad that I decided to go for this, especially at such a trying time in my life. Now that Jayson's true colors are out in the open, I can't imagine how disappointed I'd feel knowing that I let this chance pass me by, especially for the sake of appeasing him. This is the exact pick me up I need. Just as I type up my reply and hit send, Jade and Kara walk into the restaurant and join me at our table. I instantly stand up and greet them with hugs. They knew that I finally dumped Jayson. After sharing the horrifying details, they were more than willing to be there for me while I sorted through my feelings.

"Are you alright?" Kara asks.

We all take our seats, and I quickly nod.

"Surprisingly yes. It's weird, but after finally

accepting where I stand with him it was easy to walk away," I say.

Jade says, "Well if it means anything, I'm really proud of you girl. I know this is a big change, but we're here for you."

"Thanks, guys. I really appreciate you both for being by my side during all these ups and downs. I know I had to have frustrated and annoyed the hell out of you with being so naïve. But I'm so done with all that," I say.

They both smile.

I continue, "Plus, I learned that my intuition is a hell of a thing. I swear I will never ignore that shit again!"

"Hallelujah!" Kara adds.

We all share a laugh as the waitress greets us at our table and asks to take our order. After we put in our request for our usual coffee, French toast, and omelets dishes, I clear my throat.

"I have more good news," I smile.

"We're listening!" Jade replies.

I say, "I decided to take that teaching job in India. I leave in three weeks."

Jade's eyes light up, "Oh my God! That's amazing!"

"Yes, Blair! The glow-up has officially begun!" Kara boasts.

I laugh, "The glow-up? What's that?"

"Girl! It's what happens when you stop dealing with shitty men! Once you kick them to the curb a bunch of blessings comes your way. Your skin starts glowing, and your hair starts flowing. It's a real thing, look it up," she explains as if she's an expert.

I chuckle at her rationalization, but the idea of it sounds quite appealing. Whatever it is, it feels different, hopeful. I'm more than ready to make room for new and positive experiences in my life. I'm done being sad all the time.

"Well here's to my glow-up!" I cheer.

We raise our glasses of ice water and share a toast.

After brunch, I return home, eager to embark on this new chapter in my life. As I pull into the driveway, the sight of Jayson's car startles me. Since kicking him out, I had all the locks changed and blocked him on my phone. I guess I shouldn't be surprised that he'd make one last-ditch attempt to win me back. It's always worked for him in the past, why should this time be any different? *Oh, but it was.*

I remain calm and park my car before getting out. Once he sees me, he quickly gets out and leans up against his car. He's nervous, putting his hands in his front pockets. Although it's only been a few days since we last saw one another, he looks different. The Superman luster that I once loved about him is gone. The person standing before me isn't a hero at all; he's a lost little boy that gets off on hurting others to make himself feel whole.

"What are you doing here?" I ask as I approach the home we once shared.

"I'm here to talk."

I swiftly shake my head, "There's nothing more to talk about."

"I got a promotion," Jayson continues.

"That's great. Congratulations," I reply.

Despite him being an asshole, I was happy for him. Still, that didn't change anything.

"We can finally get a bigger house and start planning for the wedding," he says.

I explain, "There is no more we Jayson. That's great for you, but we are done. There won't be a bigger house or a wedding."

He refuses to back down, "So you're really done? You're giving up on all we have?"

"You gave up on us the moment you cheated. I'm not some toy you can dick around and play with," I say.

"I made a mistake, but I promise you I'm done with Renee," he pleads.

I shake my head, amused at how easily bullshit seems to roll off of his tongue.

"Yea I bet, what about your baby?" I ask.

He puts his hand on his forehead, "I can't change that."

"How many others were there? I'm pretty sure Renee wasn't the only one," I say.

I can immediately sense his hesitation; he was a fool if he didn't expect me to ask sooner or later. He remains silent and looks down at the pavement, telling me everything I needed to know. I can't lie, fully grasping the truth hurts.

I question, "Did you ever love me? Was any of it real?"

He quickly states, "Yes I love you! How can you ask

that?"

I shake my head, "You have a fucked up idea of what loving someone is."

Jayson sighs, "Maybe I do. I'm sorry I lied to you. You deserve better, and I'll do better. Please give me another chance."

"You're always sorry, and always trying to make up for your mistakes. How about stop being a deceitful, lying bastard? Then you won't have anything to be sorry for," I answer.

Jayson pries, "How can you walk away from all the time we have together? We've been together eight years, does that mean nothing to you?"

I shake my head, "No, not anymore. We're done, Jayson. The woman I am has no business being with someone like you. I know now that I deserve better. You seriously need help. I don't know how you can look yourself in the mirror, knowing how you treat people."

I can tell that my words sting. But when I look at him, I see nothing more than an insecure man that is incapable of loving me the way I ought to be loved.

"So what? You think you're perfect? What makes you so much better than me?" he argues.

I snort, "You know what? Maybe I am."

My confidence shocks him. He isn't used to me being able to stand my ground. By now his begging and manipulation would normally work on me and bring my guard down. Not today, not anymore.

I turn and walk towards the front door. He stands there, dumbfounded and at a loss of words. But I wasn't done. I stop and approach him once more.

"Oh yea, I decided to take that teaching job. I've been waiting to tell you and figured we could work through it like everything else. I hate that I allowed you to make me feel like I had to choose, especially because I would never do that to you. I never had a problem with supporting you and your dreams. It's a shame that you couldn't do the same for me. Thank God I finally woke the hell up and chose myself for once. I will never give you that power again," I say.

His eyes grow red, and I can tell he's panicked.

"How does it feel to be lied to?"

He's mute again, further proving my point. This man has nothing else to offer me.

I roll my eyes and walk up the steps towards the door, "I'll let you know when you can come by and get the rest of your stuff. Goodbye Jayson."

Once inside, I swiftly close the door and lock it behind me. Sounds of Jayson's car come through the house and I peek out the blinds to watch him pull away. Relief settles in, and I wonder why in the hell it took me so long to do that. It felt magnificent.

The next day, I'm in my studio mixing different colors to create the perfect shade of orange, my favorite color. My hair is wild and tossed into a loose bun; I'm barefoot wearing only a muscle shirt and panties. My legs and arms are covered with various colors of paint, and I couldn't be happier. Sage burns in the background as the voice of Alina Baraz sets the mood and helps me vibe out. I want to cleanse my spirit and focus on the positive. I was back in my zone, and the creativity was flowing out of me like hot lava.

I return to my new piece, a young black girl with an enormous kinky Afro. All of her dreams and aspirations filled her hair, her future looks bright, and her eyes are big and adventurous. She was the younger version of myself, fiery and eager to take on the world. Just as I finish putting the last touches on her, my cell rings and I quickly wipe off my hands to answer it.

"Hello?" I say.

"Hi, is this Blair Montgomery?" an unfamiliar voice asks.

I reply, "Yes this is."

"My name is Ryan Andrews; I'm with Kline and Associates. I'm calling to discuss the terms of a Louise Montgomery's will. Do you have time to meet later today or tomorrow?" he explains.

"Yes, I can come in today."

"Ok great. My office is at ten Penn Square, suite number eight," Ryan says.

I write down the information before hanging up. I shower in a hurry and reach for a change of clothes. Once dressed in a pair of jeans and old college sweatshirt, I grab my denim jacket, Louis Vuitton bag and head out of the door.

At the office, Mr. Andrews greets me with a firm handshake before asking me to take a seat on his oversized leather sofa. His office is modest but stylish; I look around admiring the artwork on his walls. He takes a seat at his desk before pulling out a manila folder and sifting through various documents.

"So Blair, I understand Louise was your grandmother," he says.

I nod, "Yes."

"I have a copy of her will here, were you aware that she had one?" he asks.

I shake my head, "No I wasn't."

He hands me a copy, and I quickly scan it.

"When did she do this?" I ask.

"A few months back," Mr. Andrews answers. "Feel free to take a couple of moments to review it in its entirety."

I read Gran's handwriting, and my heart pounds. It's as if I can hear her voice in my head. As I read the last couple of lines, my eyes grow big with surprise. My grandmother turned everything over to me, with the promise that I'd live my life to the fullest. I re-read her last words to me and can't stop the tears from falling. I smile before wiping them away in an attempt to keep my composure.

Mr. Andrews smiles before offering me a tissue. I reach for the tissue box, grabbing two and dotting my face.

He then slides another piece of paperwork in front of me, "I just need you to sign here, and we can have this all processed and transferred to you by next week."

I nod and read through the document. My eyes want

to jump out of its sockets when I see the words *"one hundred twenty-six thousand dollars"* in the fine print.

The grass is still a little wet from the melting snow. The earth around her grave is beginning to settle in, and my heart breaks. I want to stop and go back to my car, but I continue forward. There, in a space between her husband and only son lies my amazing grandmother. I neatly place the white roses I picked up on top of the family tombstone.

"Hey Gran, hey dad, hey Pop," I whisper. "Sorry, it took me so long to come see you guys."

Gran and I used to come here to see my father and Pop, but knowing that she was now with them is tough to stomach. Truth be told, I've been avoiding this day since laying Gran to rest. Seeing her place in the grave makes it all too real.

"I got your message; I promise you that I won't let any of you down. I miss you all so much. I'll make you guys proud."

There's a slight breeze that tickles my skin, causing me to grin.

"I'm going to India Gran, and after that, who knows. But I think it's time that I see the world like you've been telling me to do," I say.

I remain silent and stare at the ground before slowly reaching into my coat pocket and pulling out a piece of paper. I can feel my heart race, and my eyes start to water.

After taking a few deep breaths to calm my nerves, I say, "I wrote something I thought you'd like."

I recite, *"Beautiful black girl,*
Why are you crying?
Don't you know your power?
Can't you see your light?
Others tried to count you out.
Silly them! They don't know what you're about.
So dry your eyes and stay in this fight.
You have a strength they can never take from you.
You're the sunshine in this life."

I can hear birds chirping, and it briefly interrupts my train of thought. I smile and imagine that it's my Gran talking back to me. Moments later, I kiss the granite headstone before hugging it tightly and returning to my car.

10

A week later, I pull up to the middle school, eager to see my students. It's been almost a month since I taught and I missed them dearly. As I approach the classroom, I can hear them laughing and joking with one another, being their usual silly selves. I hate that I would be leaving them so soon, but I know that they are being left in good hands.

As soon as I open the door and they see that it's me, their faces light up. They all rush over to me at once, greeting me with hugs and an abundance of questions. I smile and encourage them to take their seats as I walk over to my desk. I'm surprised to see a large hand-painted card. When I open it, I'm touched to see that all of my students signed it, showering me with their love and support since my Gran passed.

I look up and can't fight back the tears, "You guys are my best students. Thank you so much."

"We love you too Ms. Montgomery!" they say.

I quickly wipe my eyes, "I have something to tell you all."

The classroom grows quiet with anticipation.

I exhale, "I have been given an opportunity to go away for a few months to teach kids like you all about art and how dope it is. I'll be leaving this week, but it's only for a short while. Ms. Childs will be teaching you for the remainder of the year, and she is pretty amazing. I promise I'll be back in time for next school year if you guys will have me."

I can see the sadness written all over their faces and my heart breaks. Leaving them was the hardest part of my new beginning.

Without saying a word, Yesenia gets up from her seat and hugs me, "We understand Ms. Montgomery. We'll be here when you get back."

One by one, my students follow suit. Some joking, some crying, but they are all supportive. I can't help but be amazed at their maturity. After drying our eyes, I let them put on their favorite music, and we dig into my lesson for the day.

Back at home, I hop into the shower and wash the girl I've been for so long out of my system and out of my life. I'm ready to live. I'm ready to be who I was truly. I scrub away the hurt, the pain, the lies, the deceit, and all things that became common in my life for far too long. I emerge from the shower feeling brand new.

I walk up to my vanity mirror and wrap my towel around my body. I stare back at myself and examine every inch of my being. I twirl my wet curls in my hands and smile, before shooting Tania a quick text requesting a hair appointment.

I put the last of my belongings in storage and can't believe the time has finally come. Tomorrow is the day; I'd be leaving for India. The last few days have been an absolute whirlwind. Between finding someone to sublease the condo and packing up all my things, I was looking forward to getting together with my friends for one last hoorah. After meeting up with my new tenants and giving them the keys, I hop into my car and head to Kara's. To celebrate, she insisted on having dinner at her house and offered to take me to the airport in the morning.

I walk into her house, and the entire gang is there, including Jade's parents, her sister Aleena and husband, Jared. As soon as I step into the living room, everyone's jaw drops.

"Oh, my goodness Blair! Your hair!" Jade exclaims.

All of their eyes are wide with shock. I guess seeing my new haircut is a lot to digest. I smile and greet them all with a warm hug. Although I kept some of my curls on top, I convinced Tania to get rid of the dead weight I've carried around with me for far too long. I realized that I clung to my hair like I did my relationship. I viewed them both as my security blankets, and I allowed fear of the unknown and change to cripple me. But not anymore. As a result, my hair was tapered and low on both sides with honey blond streaks. I love my new look and never felt more liberated.

"I'm feeling it!" Kai says before giving me a warm hug.

"Me too!" Kara adds, "The glow-up is real girl. I see you!"

I greet everyone with hugs before we all take our seats at Kara's luxurious dining table. The spread is an impressive array of Italian food and delicious wine.

"Alight now Blair, don't be eating all that pork and whatnot over there. You may come home without a booty hole," Cliff, Jade's dad jokes.

We all erupt with laughter as her mother Michelle, Jade's mother, gently nudges him in his side. She doesn't hide that she's embarrassed by her husband's candor. They're back from their recent vacation in Hawaii. Both look visibly tanned and so adorably happy together. Suddenly, Aleena stands up holding a glass of water and we all quiet down.

"Blair, I just want to congratulate you on this new journey in your life. I've always looked at you as a second older sister. Whoever Jade loves, I love. We will love and miss you while you're gone and wish you many blessings!" she beams.

I smile and rise to kiss her on the cheek. Her words mean a lot to me. I can remember her being young and trying to follow Jade and me around everywhere. As she talks, it dawns on me that I was wrong. I'm not alone; I'm in a room full of people that love me and are in my corner, they're my family.

She continues, "With everyone being here tonight, Jared and I have some exciting news to share."

Jared quietly stands up and takes his wife's hand.

"We're pregnant!" she announces.

At once we are overtaken by joy and excitement.

Jade is ecstatic and rushes over to her sister's side, "I'm going to be an auntie!"

The two hug and I can see her parents are equally happy and excited. The night couldn't be more perfect. We all share laughs and talk about the future ahead. By the end of the evening, everyone is full and pretty exhausted. One by one, they trickle out giving me their best wishes.

Jade hugs me, "I'm so sad that you won't be here for my birthday!"

"I'll make it up to you, I promise," I smile.

"You better hooch," she jokes.

Jade gives me another big hug. We stand there holding one another for a long while, both unwilling to let go.

She whimpers, "I'm going to miss you so much."

"Me too."

"Please take care of yourself out there," she pleads.

I smile, "I will."

When we finally let go, we're both in tears.

She wipes her eyes, and we hug once more, "I love you."

"Love you more," I say.

"See you, Blair," Max says, giving me a warm hug.

"Make sure you take care of my girl," I order.

He winks, "I got you."

I knew that he would and knowing that made leaving her easier to bear. The two take hands and leave after saying their goodbyes to Kara and Kai. Kai stays behind, helping Kara and I clean and wash the dishes. By the end of the night, Kara is visibly exhausted and retreats to her bedroom. I pour what's left of the wine into my glass and walk out onto her living room balcony. I lean onto the rail and admire the evening stars. Moments later, Kai joins me outside.

He brushes up next to me, "So, are you excited to be leaving?"

I smile and turn to face him, "Yes, I can't wait to meet the kids."

Kai smiles back, "I'm really happy for you Blair. I'm glad to see that you're doing ok."

"Thank you, Kai. Thank you for you know, being there," I say.

"Of course. I'm sure you know that I've always had a crush on you," he confesses. "You're such a beautiful person inside and out."

I look at him and for the first time really can see that he is attracted to me. I realize that a deep part of me knew it all along; if I allowed myself to admit it, I've always had an eye for him too. The epiphany makes my heart skip a beat. He leans in and softly kisses me on the lips. I welcome him into my space, kissing him back. His arms feel warm and safe, just like at Gran's funeral. Our tongues dance and the attraction makes my head spin, completely lost in his kiss. Everything about him feels so good. Suddenly, a familiar aching takes over my most private parts, and I gasp.

"Wait," I say, pushing him back.

"What's wrong?"

I quickly shake my head, "Nothing. You're perfect; but I'm not ready for this."

"Oh," he says, looking a little defeated. "I'm sorry, I understand."

I stop him, "No, don't be. I like you, Kai, if I'm being honest with myself, I always have. But you know I just got out of a situation, that and you're one of my best friend's brothers. I don't want to rush into anything with you."

"I respect that. Take all the time you need," he says.

His understanding means a lot to me. I feel like the old me would've jumped head first into starting something with him. But over the last few weeks, being alone and learning how to enjoy my own company has been something I've grown to appreciate. I realize that before I could even think about pursuing anything with Kai, or anyone for that matter, I had to learn to love myself unconditionally first. I had so much to learn about myself: who I was, what I liked, and what I wanted.

I smile, "Thank you."

We hug once more, and he gives me a kiss on the cheek.

Kai whispers, "Good luck in India, I'll be here when you get back."

After I walk him to the door and let him out, my stomach flips. My day was extremely eventful, and I'm happy that it came to an end. I yawn and want nothing more than to catch up on some sleep before my long flight tomorrow. I head towards Kara's spare bedroom, eager to fall asleep and get lost in my dreams.

The next morning Kara and I are on our way to the airport. Kara is driving, she's unusually quiet, and I can tell that she's a little sad.

"I won't be gone forever you know," I tease.

She smiles, "I know, but I'm still going to miss you. Who am I supposed to hang with now that you're gone, and Jade's all in love?"

"Kai," I tease.

She giggles and rolls her eyes, "Girl please."

I nervously sip my coffee, "About him. Can I ask you something?"

"Y'all fucking?" she asks.

The bluntness of her question almost makes me spit my coffee out onto the dashboard of her Mercedes.

"What? No!" I squeal.

She laughs, "Relax girl; I know you guys like each other."

I'm surprised, "You do? How?"

"Because you both get those dumb ass googly eyes whenever you see each other."

I can't help but laugh.

Kara continues, "But seriously, I think you two should go for it. Don't let me stop you. Shit if it works out, we can be sisters!"

The thought of it sounds comforting.

"Thanks, Kara, but let's not get ahead of ourselves. I need to be single and focus on myself for a while," I say.

"I understand completely," she nods.

I turn to her. There was something I've been meaning to say for the last few weeks. She notices and eyes me with suspicion.

"What's up?" she asks.

I confess, "I'm sorry if you ever thought I was being too hard or judgmental. You're my friend, and I only want the best for you. I know it may not always seem that way, but I worry about you."

Kara is surprised by my confession but seems touched, "I really appreciate that. But don't you worry about me; I promise I'll be fine. You just focus on living out your dreams and enjoying it."

I take her hand and enjoy the comfortable silence. A few minutes later, we pull up to the airport and my heart races. *This is it.* Deep down, I know that I'm ready. After Kara parks, we both get out, and she helps me with my bags.

Kara says, "Make sure you call when you can!"

"Of course girl. I'll be back before you know it," I reply.

"I know."

We share a long hug.

"I'm so proud of you Blair," she whispers.

I nod and try to fight back my tears. After a moment we finally let go.

She wipes her eyes and snaps her fingers, "You better slay India too! Take plenty of pictures!"

I laugh, "Now you know I will!"

We share one last hug before I grab my bags. I turn around and enter the airport, leaving behind the girl I once was and ready to take on my new life.

KARA

I carefully put my lipstick on and give my hair one last fluff. After securing the bra strap to my cherry lace teddy I reach for my silk robe, both surprise gifts left for me at the receptionist. I take a sip of my Dom Perignon, another gift, and admire what I see in the mirror. Just as I finish putting on my red patent leather stilettos, I hear a soft knock at my hotel door.

The mood is set with Avant playing in the background and an array of ivory candles burning by the bed. I never knew how much I liked staying at fancy hotels. If you think about it, there is something sexy about being in a new place, where no one knows you. You're free to be whomever you please. I open the door, and his seductive eyes slowly trail up my body. The fire within me is already ignited. He licks his lips, and the right corner slightly turns up. *That drives me crazy!* I step aside and let him in.

As soon as he closes the door he's all over me, his hands caressing every inch of my body, softly squeezing my thighs and behind. I sling my arms around his neck and kiss him deeply; I can taste the peppermint on his tongue. Even though it's only been a few hours since I last saw him, I wanted him badly. He leads me towards the bed, but I stop him and softly push him up against the wall. He's surprised but turned on by my aggression. The smell of his Tom Ford cologne instantly makes me moist between my legs. I yank at his suit and tug off his expensive suit jacket. I've always appreciated a man that could wear a suit (and he definitely can), but I want nothing more than to get rid of it. I undo his tie and unbutton his shirt in a hurry before reaching for his belt buckle and unzipping his tailored pants.

I take his length into my hands and gently caress it. The more I touch, the harder it grows. He weaves his fingers into my hair before pulling me into another kiss. I let my tongue slowly trail his lips before stepping back and getting down onto my knees. Without hesitation, I hungrily take him into my mouth. He closes his eyes and tilts his head back while I go to work. I moan and enjoy the way he tastes. He watches me with desire in his eyes. *Gosh he's so sexy!*

"Pick up that tie," he instructs.

I bite my bottom lip and do as I'm told before sliding onto the bed. He kicks off his pants and gently takes my arms. I smile as he kisses me once more. Then, he wraps his silver tie around my wrists and secures it to the headboard. He kisses and licks all over my body, slowly allowing his tongue and hands to caress and suck on my breasts, pushing my nerves over the edge. By the time he's done teasing me, I'm begging to feel him inside of me. He smirks, pleased with his work, and slowly enters my body. I swear that I feel like I'm flying. He holds my legs open as he strokes me like an expert and I feel my explosion building. Every inch of his manhood has taken over me; I cry out as he continuously hits my G-spot. I raise my hips, meeting his thrusts. Suddenly, he unties my hands and flips me over to my stomach, pulling me up onto my knees. I gasp as he enters me from behind. I bite into the plush white pillow as he takes a handful of my hair and kisses my neck.

"This pussy is mine," he whispers.

That was enough to send me over the moon. We both explode together, and he crashes into my back before we fall asleep in each other's arms. The next morning, I hear the shower going. I roll over and check my clock. I had to get up soon to catch my flight back to Philadelphia. As I sit up, he comes out looking as sexy as ever. I never thought I'd be attracted to an older man, but he wasn't like anyone else. The fact that he was my boss made the entire ordeal that much more erotic. He leans in and gives me a tender kiss.

"Good morning," he says.

I smile and watch him as he gets dressed.

"This was fun," I say.

"Indeed it was," he smirks and finishes zipping up his pants. "Until next time."

We kiss once more before he lets himself out. He leaves to go back to his life, and his wife while I hop out of bed, eager to return to mine.

Stay tuned for *Dilemmas of a Damsel: Part III* coming Summer 2018!

LET'S CONNECT!

 **@Author Monique Elise**

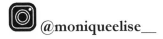 **@moniqueelise__**

 **@iammoniqueelise**

 **@Monique Elise**

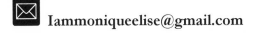 **Iammoniqueelise@gmail.com**

Join my mailing list at www.moniqueelise.com for all the latest news, updates, and exclusive sneak peeks!

If you liked this book, please leave a review on Amazon and Goodreads!

ABOUT THE AUTHOR

Monique Elise is a blogger who currently resides in Philadelphia, Pennsylvania. A native of Reading, Pa, she fell in love with writing and literature at a young age. Growing up, she would frequent the library with her mother and get lost in various books for days at a time. Her favorites authors include Omar Tyree and Eric Jerome Dickey. After finishing high school, she went on to earn her Bachelor of Business Administration in Finance from Temple University and MBA from Rosemont College. With the support and encouragement of her family and friends, Monique ventured into the world of freelance blogging. She discovered how much she loved sharing her thoughts and opening a panel for discussion with her readers. In 2017, she decided to launch her own lifestyle and dating blog moniqueelise.com to connect with her readers and while discussing topics modern and ambitious women can relate to.

Made in the USA
Columbia, SC
11 April 2018